# THE FINISH LINE

## A TOWER CITY ROMANCE TRILOGY SEQUEL
## NOVELLA

### VANIA RHEAULT

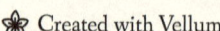 Created with Vellum

# IAN

Ian Butler held the phone to his ear.

"Yeah, thanks for the opportunity. No, it wasn't too late. Still at the bar. Yeah, yeah. Goodnight."

He sat in The Finish Line's tiny office and instead of hanging up, he tapped the receiver against his lips.

Things have been going well. Maybe too well.

When things went up, they always came down.

The news didn't have to be bad. Depended on his perspective. And the others'.

Brett and Dane weren't always on steady ground, and this news might be welcome.

Ian pushed away from the little desk crammed full of family photos. The largest, the one that should be hanging on the wall, was of the six of them at The Finish Line's grand opening last year. Their first dollar spent, framed by the Tower City's Chamber of Commerce, hung behind his head.

That dollar represented a lot to Ian. Maybe more to him than Brett and Dane. Brett started the Tower City

Marathon from nothing, and Dane opened his running shoe store without anyone's help.

But The Finish Line, the bar and grill was Ian's baby.

He upholstered booths. Waxed wood until it shined.

And he served the first drink behind the bar he would always think of as his, no matter who slung drinks at night.

After hours, The Finish Line was empty now but for the cook they'd hired to run the kitchen. Crashes and bangs sounded through the wall as Bobbi Avery set things to right for the next day.

"I'm heading out, boss," she said, poking her head into the office.

She still looked bright after ten hours on the job, and he envied her the amount of energy she still had at three in the morning. The late nights weren't new to him but sitting in an empty bar was a lot different than serving drinks to a packed house until closing time.

"I won't be long after you. Drive safely."

"You, too."

After Bobbi left, Ian turned off the lights and locked up. He didn't need to be in the next day until later.

The three of them ran a tight ship, their schedules a finely tuned balancing act.

No one put in more effort than the others, and no one worked longer hours than the others. Everyone worked their 33.33% and not one percentile more.

To work together peacefully no one could feel cheated and for the past eighteen months, it had worked in their favor. They had no intention to run The Finish Line any other way.

Unless they didn't run it at all.

Ian sighed and drove home.

He'd never get tired of the sound when he thought of it. Home. To his girls. Maybe another man would crumble under the amount of estrogen under his roof, but not him. He thrived.

Marta in his bed, soft and waiting for him. Shyla sleeping in a toddler bed in their room. Likely, the little girl would be snuggled into Marta's side and he'd have to move her, only to find the tiny scamp wedged between them come morning.

He didn't mind.

Ian parked in the driveway of the house he'd purchased in a quiet, residential neighborhood. A dog barked down the street, and a light shined upstairs. Sadie must be feeding Hannah. The baby still liked to wake up for a snack if she was going through a growth spurt.

No, he had no complaints. He counted his blessings every day.

Marta left the light burning over the stove in the kitchen, and it kept him from tripping over a stray doll lying in the middle of the floor.

He scooped it up and dumped it into a massive toy box in the corner of the living room. Unbuttoning his shirt and loosening his tie, he took the stairs and peered into Sadie's room.

She rocked Hannah in a small recliner, the baby gripping a bottle that was almost empty.

"You okay?" he whispered. "Need help?"

He kept his voice low. Hannah loved him and he joked she was his little shadow. She would wake if she knew he'd come home from work.

"I'm okay. We'll go back to bed soon."

"Okay. Night."

"Night."

Sadie had grown out her hair, and now the blonde color matched the baby's tousled curls.

People asked if Sadie's happy leap into motherhood surprised him. He never said he thought she would have a hard time because he didn't want his doubts to become fact, but in the back of his mind he'd been prepare—he and Marta both. Their caution had been unwarranted, and he would always be grateful Sadie loved Hannah with everything she had. She balanced being a mother and a student with an aplomb he could only admire.

It was true she had a lot of help. Nikki babysat on occasion, and Alyssa stepped in a few times, too. Hannah idolized Drew, toddling along after him whenever they were together. Sadie swore the girl took her first steps chasing after a boy.

Uncle Ian would cross that bridge no sooner than in eighteen years, though Brett already had the two married and having a family of their own. Something Ian didn't appreciate, but he went along with the joke it was.

Ian made his way into his dark bedroom. A small nightlight lit up the corner of the room.

Shyla slept in her toddler bed pushed against the wall under the window. She'd never taken to her own room, preferring to sleep near Marta. His parents warned them they would regret it later, but he and Marta would work it out when the time came. If it did. Shyla exhibited independence in every other facet of her life. Nighttime would follow. Maybe not soon, but he wasn't in any rush for her to grow up.

He stripped the rest of his clothes and climbed into bed. When he'd finally convinced Marta to stay, when she'd finally moved in, he'd had some of the happiest moments of his life.

Cooking together, doing chores. Mowing while she played with Shyla in her sandbox.

He'd been born a family man and crawling into bed with her was the highlight of his day.

After a hard, honest day's work, there wasn't anything better than slipping between crisp sheets and pulling her to him.

Since she stopped her grueling training schedule, she'd filled out, and he loved her soft curves.

As she sighed softly in her sleep, he spooned her, slipping his hand under her pajama tank top and cupping the full swell of her breast.

Her smooth skin made him instantly hard, and he turned her onto her back, taking her mouth with his.

He didn't want to wake Hannah or Shyla, but he had no qualms about waking Marta, making love to her in the middle of the night.

"Did you have a good day?" she asked against his mouth.

"I did. We all did. I heard some news."

"About the girls?"

"About The Finish Line."

Marta pulled away. "Bad?"

"No."

He hadn't given up her breast, and he squeezed, grinning against her lips as her nipple hardened under his touch.

She moaned.

He trailed his hand over her ribs, and she whimpered in disappointment.

"Patience, my love." He brushed his thumb against her skin. "Marta, are you happy?"

She lifted her hand to his face. He was past having a five

o'clock shadow, but she loved it, and he skipped shaving just for her.

"Have I hurt you so much you still have to ask?"

She had hurt him, running from his love, from the family he wanted to give her. She'd had her reasons, but they hadn't stopped him from waking in a cold sweat for weeks after she'd moved in, expecting his bed to be empty.

Gradually, he'd been able to sleep through the night. To not panic if he woke and she wasn't in bed, maybe in the kitchen instead, making coffee, or in the rocking chair holding Shyla as the sun came up.

While he'd stopped worrying she would disappear, that didn't mean he would ever take her for granted, and he checked in with her frequently, making sure she had what she needed. From him, from their relationship.

And she did the same for him.

"No. Making sure."

"You know what would make me happy?"

"What's that?" He nuzzled her lips with his and found the waistband of her sleep shorts. His fingers slid past the silky thatch of hair and found her wet and willing.

"Make love to me." She gasped when he pushed a finger inside her.

"That's the plan."

She pulled her tank top off, and he eased her shorts from her legs. Her ankle had healed, but not as completely as they'd hoped. Even after eighteen months she still nursed it.

And though she put on one of the Midwest's largest marathons, she never ran again.

When her pajamas were on the floor, he pulled the covers over their heads.

"You want to suffocate me?" she asked, nibbling his

neck, her hands gliding over his skin.

He settled between her legs, his cock thick and heavy. The tip nudged her, and she widened her thighs.

"I don't want to wake Shyla," he said, pushing into her.

She muffled a moan, and he raised her hips with a hand under her ass.

For a long time he couldn't make love to her without worrying about her *thinking* things. Baby things.

Not for herself, but for him.

Yeah, he wanted to be a dad. Out of bed, it had taken several rounds with her to make her believe that every time Shyla called him "Daddy" he already was. It didn't matter where the babies came from.

It had only taken once in a heated night of lovemaking to make her understand that his violent craving for her went beyond procreation. He needed to touch her, he needed to feel her under him, her legs wrapped around his waist, keeping him close.

He needed to hear, after he told her he loved her, that she loved him, too.

Heat coiled in his belly, but he backed off to find her clit. He wanted her with him. They would always be together, in every way possible.

Marta panted as he circled her sensitive skin with the tip of his finger. "Ian."

"I love you, Marta. You gotta tell me you'll never leave me."

"Oh, sweetheart."

He thrust as his finger slipped between them one last time, and she went over, her muscles clutching at him as he spurted inside her.

Gasping for breath, he threw the comforter aside and sucked in the fresh air.

Marta was right. He almost suffocated them. Holy shit.

He lowered himself onto her, their bodies covered in sweat, but he didn't pull out of her, not yet.

Whenever he did, he felt like half of him went missing.

"Ian," her words whispered over his skin, "I'm never going to leave you."

She ran her fingers through his hair, wiped away the perspiration at his temples.

He hugged her to him, crushing her breasts against his chest. Nibbling at her mouth, he kissed her until she had to pull away to breathe.

"Marry me," he said, meeting her eyes in the glow from the nightlight.

"I already said I would."

"But, we're not yet. You didn't let me buy you a ring."

That was a tender subject between them. She said they needed every penny for clothes for Shyla, her daycare expenses. The mortgage. The Finish Line.

He said he wanted to make her his in every way possible, and they'd compromised. He bought her a necklace she never took off.

She ran her toes along the back of one of his calves. "We've been busy."

An unexplained urgency hit him like a ton of bricks. Maybe it had to do with the call. Maybe it had to do with remembering what the first few months of their relationship had been like. When he still hadn't been sure if she'd stay.

Or maybe it had to do with how much he simply loved her and wanted his ring on her finger. Wanted her name on the adoption papers, making her Shyla's mother, legally.

"Soon," he mumbled into her hair. "Soon."

"Soon," she said, nipping at his jaw, making him hard all over again.

# ALYSSA

Alyssa Barnes stared at her computer screen.

A half-finished novel blinked at her, but she was too on-edge to write anymore tonight. She wanted to be Alyssa Sommers by now, but Drew came along. Nikki and Dane married in a large wedding that took months to plan, and Brett's time had been tied up with opening The Finish Line.

The hard work paid off, and The Finish Line had turned into one of the most popular hangouts in Tower City.

But lately something had shifted, and things felt more "off" than "on" for lack of a better way to explain it. Brett had never been particularly restful, buzzing with energy that wasn't always positive, and her becoming pregnant so soon into their relationship didn't help.

Eighteen months later, she was sure Brett didn't want to be with her anymore.

Drew slept in a crib she'd set up in her loft allowing her to write during nap time and into the early morning hours while she waited for Brett to come home after closing the bar.

The baby slept in the wooden crib now, his soft breaths a slow rhythm that soothed her heart.

Maybe having a baby hadn't been right for her and Brett as a couple, but it had been right for *her*. She loved her little boy. Even if in the end she'd sacrificed her relationship with the man she fought so hard to love.

The door downstairs opened and shut. Keys rattled on the counter where Brett always threw them when he came home.

He plodded up the stairs, his tread heavy. It had been his turn to close the bar, the time slipping past three in the morning.

Alyssa stiffened, but he never failed to take her breath.

He wore a dress shirt, tie, and dress slacks. He looked different than when they'd met. Back then he'd worn his running clothes everywhere he went, but he didn't run much anymore. What little free time he had he spent with her and Drew.

"Hey," she murmured, the word close to sticking in her mouth.

She didn't want to wake Drew, but more than that, she didn't want to speak to Brett. She was terrified of what he would say back.

He confirmed her suspicions. Looking at her, the crib where his son lay, out the window into the pre-dawn night, he shifted from foot to foot and finally said, "This isn't working for me."

She fought not to lash out.

He didn't deserve it.

She'd been the one to convince him to have a baby. It wasn't his fault her pregnancy had been difficult and

Drew's delivery a traumatic experience for them all. It wasn't his fault they hadn't had sex since Drew's birth because it hurt her, and only now, a year later, she felt like she was slowly getting her body back.

After their baby's birth, her doctor diagnosed her with a horrible case of postpartum depression. Part of the problem was her weight gain. Over the past year she hadn't felt good enough to work out, and she hadn't lost any of the baby pounds she'd gained while pregnant.

Probably the only reason Brett hadn't walked out on her up until now was the fact Drew was an easy baby. He slept through the night, didn't have any ear infections, nursed without latching problems, then took to a bottle at nine months without any issues.

He couldn't have handled a fussy baby.

For the first two months after their baby's birth, her mother had come to help. While she and Brett put aside their differences, every once in a while the animosity between them would be too much, and he'd spend more than his allotted time at The Finish Line.

Her mother hadn't forgiven him for the rocky start of their relationship, and that made him bitter because for the past eighteen months he'd given her and Drew everything he had.

It wiped him out.

So now, when he announced their new status quo wasn't working, it didn't surprise her.

What did was his timing.

She'd expected it a lot sooner than this.

"I know."

He rubbed his son's back for a moment before sinking into the rocking recliner Alyssa moved upstairs to nurse Drew while she took writing breaks.

Leaning back, he closed his eyes. "I pictured different things," he murmured.

She stared at the screen and tried to keep her voice steady. "I did, too. I'm sorry."

Without meeting her eyes, he said, "It's not your fault."

*Not her fault?*

Of course it was. She'd insisted on getting pregnant when she knew he wasn't ready.

They spent the advance from their running manual on The Finish Line. Instead they could have taken a vacation, a childless vacation, gotten to know each other. Or put the money toward a house.

It was too late for all of that.

Because of her impatience, Brett found himself in a situation he didn't want to be in.

All this was entirely her fault.

But she could fix it.

"When are you leaving?" she asked.

Put that out there. If he wanted to move out, she wanted him to do it as soon as possible. Maybe it wouldn't hurt so much then.

He cracked his eyes open. They glittered hard in her monitor's glow. *"What?"*

"Leaving. Moving out." She paused. "Drew stays with me. We'll figure out visitation through a family attorney, I guess. Since we're not married."

Brett sprang from the chair, and Alyssa reared back, her heart leaping into her throat.

Drew shifted in his sleep.

"Are you kicking me out?" he asked, his chest heaving.

She gripped the armrests of her desk chair until her knuckles ached. "You mean you weren't talking about leaving?"

"No!" He grimaced and shot a quick look at the sleeping little boy. "No. Why would you think that? Do you want me to go? I know things haven't been . . ."

She waited. She wanted to see how he would describe the last year.

"I haven't been here for you the way I should have. The way I promised I would be. The way I've wanted to be."

He sank to his knees in front of her and pressed his face into her belly.

She ran her fingers through his hair.

"I miss you and Drew."

Her muscles relaxed and the tension drained out of her. "You meant The Finish Line."

Brett lifted his head. "Of course I meant The Finish Line. What did you think I meant?"

"Me."

"That's how messed up the last year and a half have been. We're not on the same page. You and Drew are the best things to happen to me. I need more time with you. I missed his entire first year because I spent fourteen fucking hours a day at the bar getting it off the ground. Now I do it because it's the place to be, and I don't want to do it anymore. I miss you."

"Why didn't you say something sooner?"

Brett's fingers dug into the flabby flesh of her midsection. "Because I didn't feel like I could. Dane and Ian never would have accomplished what we have without my help. At least, not so soon."

She hugged him to her. "I didn't know you felt that way."

"I didn't want to complain, but I missed Drew's first tooth, his first word. His first steps. I need more, Alyssa. Before it's too late. I hope you understand."

"I do, but it's not up to me."

"Dane and Ian aren't going to like what I have to say, and I don't want that to cause problems for you with Nik and Marta."

"I think that's the least of our worries if you really want Dane and Ian to buy you out."

He blew out a breath. "Let's run away. Stay in Florida with your parents. Drew can chase birds on the beach. Let your mom babysit and we'll spend time together. Just us. No stress, no exhaustion. I want to make love to you. I've missed you in all the ways I can miss you."

"I'm sorry it's been so long." She wanted to make love too, and they'd tried a couple of times. Her body had still been healing, and the way she looked was too reminiscent of the way her body had been before she started running.

He opened her robe and lifted the satin nightgown she wore underneath. Nikki bought it for her after Drew's birth. She said she still wanted Alyssa to look pretty and after a difficult delivery, it helped. Washing her hair, putting on a bit of makeup, wearing real clothes instead of pajamas, it helped.

But that didn't mean she wanted him looking at her.

"Brett. I don't think—"

"Let me touch you. I won't hurt you."

She wanted him to touch her, but she didn't want him grossed out by the way she looked.

"Please?"

Another minute went by. "Okay."

She lifted her ass a little to give him room to pull up the nightgown and slip her godawful granny-panties from her chubby thighs.

It always amazed her that he could love her while she looked like this. When he could have his choice from the bevy of busty brunettes that hung around marathon head-quarters.

The alliteration made her smile, and as Brett nudged her into the chair, desire pooled in her belly. It had been a long time since she felt it. The want of his hands on her.

As he pushed the nightgown farther up, over her breasts, she pushed back the shame.

They hung heavier now, lined with deep blue veins. He took a nipple into his mouth, and she gasped. "God."

"I used to get jealous watching you feed our son. I wanted to be where he was, sucking on you, giving you pleasure." He tugged on her other nipple.

"Brett."

"Shh." He whispered his lips over all her stretch marks, fierce and red; some still hadn't faded to the silvery-white she hoped for. "You are so beautiful. You grew our son right here," he said against her skin, near her bellybutton. "I will never have the words to thank you for the family you've given me."

His sweet words made her forget her insecurities, and she wiped the fine sheen of tears from her eyes.

Kissing lower, he paused. "I don't want to hurt you, Alyssa. You'll tell me if I do?"

"What hurt me was thinking when you came home from closing the bar tonight you wanted to leave me."

He gripped her thighs, met her eyes in the streaky lights of her screensaver. "We're only a year and a half in. You've got me for a lot longer than that."

For once she wasn't self-conscious about her flab hanging out, or the way her boobs rested on her gut. Brett looked at her like she was the most beautiful thing on earth, and if he could see that when he looked at her, then she would cut herself some slack.

He nudged her thighs apart and she tensed.

Not out of fear he would hurt her, but out of apprehension and anticipation. It'd been a long time.

She hadn't shaved, either, and he had to search for a moment before his fingers found her.

"This is a new version of hide and seek," he said, before lowering his head.

She laughed, but his tongue seared her, cutting her off, and she jerked away.

"Sit still."

She scooted to the edge of the chair and widened her legs.

"That's the way, baby," he said and continued to lick at her.

Slowly, he pushed a finger inside her.

She was so wet, and it felt good, though maybe still a little sore. Maybe not sore, but . . . unaccustomed to activity down there.

Pressing her head into the back of her chair, she arched into his mouth.

He added another finger and he sucked at her clit.

She came, swallowing her moan. She didn't want to wake Drew.

Brett worked at her, drawing out the last of her orgasm, until she couldn't take it anymore and she pulled away from him.

She flopped into the chair, perspiration covering her skin, her heart racing.

"Was that good for you?" he asked.

"Yeah. I needed that." She blew out a breath. "I, ah, forgot how good you are. Thanks."

Smirking, he said, "Don't thank me, return the favor."

He stood and held out his hand.

Her come dripped down her thighs as she stood on shaky legs.

When she approached the crib to bring Drew downstairs with them, Brett tugged her away. "Turn the monitor on. He'll be okay for a bit. Maybe you can ask Nikki to take him later. You're going to need a nap after staying up all night."

"Who said anything about staying up all night?"

"I did. I'm not done with you yet. Plus, Ian said he wants to meet with all of us in the morning."

"For what?" she asked, following her fiancé down the stairs.

"Beats me. He said he got a phone call and needs to talk to us. I said we'd meet him at the bar at ten before we open up for lunch."

"That doesn't sound good."

"Nope. But I'm thinking about other things right now."

Alyssa laughed and pushed him into their bedroom. She set the monitor on the nightstand to listen for their son if he woke before his parents were done playing.

She paused by the bed.

"We'll take it slow. I promise," he said, taking his clothes off.

"I know."

They made love as the spring sun came up, and his kisses chased her doubts away.

# DANE

Dane Montgomery turned off his phone's alarm before it went off and woke his wife.

He rolled over and brushed her hair from her face.

Nikki Montgomery.

He loved the sound of that.

Almost as much as he loved the woman who carried the name.

His hand lightly trailed over her shoulder to the large baby bump between them.

That he didn't love so much. The risk involved. Especially since there were two. He'd let her talk him into it though, and now at six months along there was no going back.

Her large blue eyes blinked open and a sleepy smile crossed her lips.

She could talk him into doing anything.

All she had to do was open her mouth and he agreed before she even spoke a word.

"Going for a run?" she asked.

"Yeah. I gotta blow off some steam."

The only runner in the group now, he made the time for at least a six mile run every day. Between taking care of his wife and his management duties at The Finish Line, stress weighed heavy.

"Are you okay?" Nikki asked, cradling his cheek in her palm.

"Worried about you."

"I'm okay. I feel good." She paused. "She knows what we're sacrificing to do this for her and Jack."

"It doesn't seem like enough."

She dropped her hand and the second she did, he missed her touch. He hated it when they fought. Not fighting, exactly, but having discussions that didn't go his way.

"My sister can't afford to pay us, and I wouldn't take her money even if she could. I wish . . ."

"What?"

"I wish I would have thought of being a surrogate for Stacy before I met you. Before we married. I hate this causes us problems."

He rested his hand on the babies she carried for her sister and brother-in-law. It didn't creep him out she had a part of Jack inside her. That was fine. He considered the babies only babies, and she never had Jack's sperm inside her. Two of Stacy's fertilized eggs had been implanted into Nikki's uterus with the hope one would stick.

Both of them had, much to everyone's delight but his.

One of the babies kicked under his touch.

"It would have been nice if they were ours, that's all."

He'd seen the way Drew transformed Brett. Fatherhood suited his friend.

Dane had had reservations about what kind of father Brett was going to be, but he never said anything, trusting Alyssa and Brett to know what they were doing. His worries were unfounded. Brett was an amazing dad, and Dane wanted that, too.

Now he had to wait.

Nikki would have a cesarean section in Chicago—where Stacy and Jack lived—to deliver the babies. He would drive his wife, pregnant with a boy and a girl, his niece and nephew, and he would drive her home empty-handed, leaving behind the babies she'd grown inside her for nine months.

It didn't seem fair, and he hoped she made it through as well as she kept saying she would.

He had his doubts. How could a woman not get attached to babies that her body nourished—she didn't create these babies, a Petrie dish had done that—for close to a year. Nourishing them now while she lay there, his hand caressing the place where the twins grew.

"You've been so busy with the bar. You know Brett missed a lot of Drew's first year. He complains about it all the time. I think this is good timing. When we have our own you'll be freer to enjoy your son or daughter. Or both. It's a good thing we're doing for my sister, and you know how much I love you for going along with it."

He did know. He'd just learned to keep his unhappiness to himself and only tell his therapist how giving away these two babies would make him feel. Nikki wouldn't be the only one to experience the loss as they drove away.

Leaning over, he pressed a kiss to her forehead. "Do you feel good enough to work?"

"Yeah, I'm good. You said you're meeting everyone at the bar this morning?"

"Yep. Ian said he has some news."

"You'll have to tell me what he says."

"I will. I need to get going or I won't have time to shower."

"I'm getting up soon, too. Stacy wants to video chat before I go in. They've started working on the nursery."

"Good for her."

He tried to keep the sarcasm out of his voice, but she heard it anyway and swatted at his arm as he rolled out of bed.

She did have a point about timing. By the time she healed and felt like carrying the baby they wanted to start their family, two years will have perhaps gone by. Maybe three.

Carrying the twins took a lot out of her and she tried to hide it, but if she wasn't at the store, she was watching TV with her feet propped up, or sleeping.

Maybe they'd be in a house by then.

Helping get The Finish Line off the ground hadn't given them any time to house hunt and they still lived in the apartment Nikki moved into when she took the job at the Tower City Running Company.

She loved being close to Alyssa, Brett, and Drew, but every time he stepped into the hallway, he thought of the way he let Eric manipulate him and it made him want to throw up.

He wouldn't be sad to say goodbye to the building and all the crappy memories with it.

When he came back from his run, Nikki was showered, sipping on decaf coffee, and logging off the video chat with her sister. She looked adorable in a pink maternity tunic and leggings, Princess Snowflake circling her ankles while she stood at the kitchen counter where they kept the laptop.

Stacy was a ball of nerves, possibly because she lived so far away and felt out of control. Dane resented her wanting to know Nikki's every movement, but his wife seemed to take it in stride, promising she wasn't eating junk food, exercising regularly, and not scooping the cat's litter.

She was doing everything she could to have a healthy pregnancy, and he kept his nose out of it. The shared pregnancy was between her and her sister.

He grinned, tolerated it, and spent all his time at The Finish Line.

Rubbing her belly, he kissed her. "Sorry about earlier."

"It's okay. Just a couple more months, then it will be over."

He didn't think it would be that easy, but he waved the white surrender flag and retreated to the shower.

Nikki poked her head into the bathroom to say goodbye before leaving to open the store, and the apartment was quiet as Dane dressed. It wasn't his turn to close the bar tonight, but it would be a long day.

Opening his own store had prepared him for that, and the time he spent bullshitting with Brett and Ian while they slung drinks and delivered food to packed tables made the shifts go by.

When Dane pulled into the lot, Bobbi's car was already parked next to Brett's and Ian's.

He whistled as he let himself in.

"You look like crap," he said to Brett who grinned and hugged Alyssa to him.

They sat at a table for eight in the middle of the room, carafes giving off the delicious scent of coffee.

"I finally got some this morning, so no sleep," Brett said.

"For fuck's sake," Alyssa said, her face bright red. "Tell everyone, why don't you."

"I just did. Like anyone cares." Brett laughed.

"I care," Dane said, just to be contrary.

"Nikki's bigger than a house already. You ain't getting any."

He gave Brett the finger.

Brett only laughed because he knew it was true.

Stacy didn't want them having sex even though Nikki's doctor said it was perfectly natural and safe if they wanted to be intimate. At least that was one area Nikki didn't do what her sister asked. But as the weeks went on and she grew more uncomfortable, the times they messed around were fewer and fewer, and instead of sex, they cuddled and he massaged her feet.

He tried to think of this as a practice round for the real thing.

"I'm glad you're feeling better," he said to Alyssa.

She hadn't stopped blushing and she muttered, "Thanks."

It had to be tough, everyone knowing everyone else's business. Alyssa's difficult delivery wasn't a secret, and the Alyssa Nikki and Dane knew had taken a while to come back.

"Where's Nik?" Ian asked, coming into the dining room from the kitchen sipping from a white mug.

"She had to open the store. Margie took the day off and there was nobody else. I'll fill her in later."

"Okay. We'll start in a second." Ian stood at the head of the table and waited for everyone to settle in and pour coffee.

Dane sat next to Marta who was texting on her phone. "How're you doing, kid?"

"I'm tired."

"More sex," Brett said, raising his coffee cup.

"Fuck off." Marta held back a smile.

Dane poured a cup of coffee. "Naughty. Good thing the

kids aren't around. Shyla picks up on that stuff faster than shit. She'd have the mouth of a sailor if you let her."

Marta laughed. "You're not kidding."

He propped his feet on an empty chair. "Let's do this."

Ian cleared his throat.

Dane leaned back to listen to him speak.

# IAN

Ian rested his hands on the back of a chair. "I got a call a couple nights ago. I sat on it until we could all get together. It's too bad Nikki couldn't be here, but you'll have to get her take on this, and maybe at some point we can meet at the house."

He had everyone's attention, and they stared like he was about to announce a death in the family. He was making a bigger deal out of this than he needed to.

"Out with it, man, or we'll have to open before you get it out of your mouth," Brett said, his arm around Alyssa's shoulders.

"Alright. I got a call the other night from the owner of the shopping mall. He owns a pretty big chunk of Tower City. He called me with an offer. A pretty generous offer."

Brett tipped his head back and blew out a breath. "Thank God."

Dane frowned. "What do you mean by that?"

Shrugging, Brett said, "I've been thinking about getting out. I didn't know how to tell you guys."

That was news to Ian. "How long have you felt that way?"

"Not long. I don't know. I'm burnt out. Miss my kid. Alyssa and I want to get married. We can't exactly do that when I spend all my time here."

Ian agreed with that. Brett had echoed his talk with Marta almost verbatim. He wanted to get married too, sooner than later, and he couldn't stuck behind the bar.

But.

"You want to let The Finish Line go? Now? After putting so much work into it?"

Brett met his stare head-on. "Yeah."

"Then what would you do?"

He tightened his hold on Alyssa, and she leaned into his side. "Marry my fiancée and the mother of my child. Take a honeymoon. Play with my son. Breathe. I'll figure it out as I go. Our relationship has suffered. I didn't fight my way out of hell to keep Alyssa only to lose her because I'm here all the fucking time."

Ian felt the same, but he thought Brett was missing the bigger picture.

In the somber way he had, Dane sat back and listened. His life was stalled, waiting for Nikki to give birth to her sister's kids. After she did that, what would Dane want? He probably didn't know.

The offer Jerry Overland threw at him had been overly generous. That told him one thing: The Finish Line had potential to be a long-time, big-time earner and Jerry wanted it. If Jerry thought it, then it was true. He wasn't the richest land developer in the state for nothing.

"Dane?" Ian asked.

Dane turned his mug on the table, his ankle propped on

his knee. His lips thinned, and he raised his eyes meeting Ian's questioning gaze.

"Who offered?"

"What? That doesn't matter."

"It does to me. Who made the fucking offer?"

Ian took a step back.

Dane had a nasty temper, but Nikki and his visits to his therapist made his outbursts almost non-existent.

"Jerry Overland."

Dane stood, his hands clenched into fists pushed against his thighs. "Fuck that. I'm not giving the bastard one thing."

Ian's mouth fell open. "You have something against Jerry Overland?"

"Fuck yeah, I do." Dane stormed out of the bar.

Brett scrubbed at his hair.

"What's going on?" Ian asked as Dane kicked at the sidewalk's curb in fury.

"Jerry Overland is his ex-wife's husband."

## ALYSSA

Alyssa melted against Brett's chest. Something changed in him. He seemed calmer, somehow. Maybe because they'd finally been able to make love. Maybe because he finally told his friends what he wanted. Whatever it was, she was grateful for it.

In the parking lot, Brett devoured her mouth, holding her face in his hands.

Maybe they'd scaled a mountain neither of them knew they were climbing, but they were at the top and they were sucking in the fresh air.

"See you later?" he mumbled against her lips.

"Yeah."

"What are you going to do now?"

"While Sadie's watching Drew, I should go home and nap, but I'm going to head over to the store and see Nikki for a second."

"Don't gossip long. Get some sleep." His eyes softened as he smoothed his thumb over her cheekbone.

"I will. Keep an eye on Dane?"

"Count on it. But he'll be okay."

"He didn't look okay."

After the meeting, Dane came back but disappeared into the office. He didn't hang around to say goodbye to anyone.

"Liz's husband wants to buy The Finish Line. He has a right to be pissed. If Tom started sniffing around again, I'd be pissed, too."

She scowled. The trainer she used to see had been so far from her mind the past year and a half she almost had to ask him who the hell he meant. "That's like comparing apples and oranges."

"Not from my perspective. He was after you. He knew a good thing and wanted it for himself."

"Well, Liz isn't after Dane. Far from it."

"Yeah, she is, but in a different way than what you meant. I don't believe it's a coincidence any more than he does."

"Go talk to him."

"I will, but we're gonna open soon. Wanted to have you for a minute. Go home and sleep."

"Okay. Brett."

He looked down at her, his hazel eyes clear, framed by dark blond lashes. He would always make her heart do funny things.

He kissed her, biting her bottom lip.

She moaned, wanting more.

That morning's lovemaking session had flipped a switch, and all she wanted was more. More love, more orgasms. The basic human need to reproduce swamped her. More babies.

Those would have to wait. She'd be smarter this time.

"I love you."

"And that makes me the happiest guy in the world."

Alyssa parked in the parking lot of Dane and Nikki's store.

The Tower City Running Company sat on one of the main strips of Tower City and it constantly attracted traffic, especially during this time of year.

The ninth annual Tower City Marathon was a week away.

After the meeting at the bar, Marta had gone to headquarters.

She'd taken over the race with little trouble, throwing herself into the position with everything she had. Brett had spent a lot of time showing her the ropes and it had rubbed Alyssa the wrong way, just a little bit, though wisely she'd kept it to herself.

After all, he'd helped Marta find her place in Tower City and Alyssa couldn't have been happier for her.

When her surgeon said that her ankle hadn't healed as it should have and she shouldn't risk further injury trying to run, she'd taken it in stride. They'd all held their breaths waiting for the second shoe to drop, pardon the pun, but it seemed as if Ian, Sadie, and the girls filled the hole running left.

Alyssa put Brett and Marta's past behind her the best she could and turned Marta into one of her closest friends.

She caught Nikki during a lull, and her best friend stood behind the counter guzzling water. She looked amazing for carrying two babies, statuesque, her skin glowing, like a model out of a maternity magazine.

No one would compare her to a whale.

Nikki helped her with Drew as much as she possibly could to help her heal, physically as well as mentally. It meant the world to her she had a friend she could trust.

She'd had attachment issues thinking no one could take care of Drew as well as she could, and the first few times Nikki or her mother fed him, changed him, or rocked him, letting her rest, instead of sleeping, she'd been a puddle of raw nerves and guilt.

It took a lot of talking with Brett to make her realize asking for help, and taking it, didn't make her a bad mother.

"Hey," she said, stepping up to the counter.

"Hey. Come in for some clothes?"

Alyssa considered the question. It would do her good to start exercising, but she'd talk to Brett first. If she started again, she wanted to go with him. Spending time with him, stealing kisses, him slapping her ass if she lagged behind.

Her cheeks pinked thinking about it.

He really had started something this morning.

"I know that look. And it's not about clothes."

"Stop it. If I want to get out there, I have my old stuff. I didn't toss any of it. I wanted to come in and warn you."

Nikki lowered her water bottle. "Is this about the meeting?"

"Yeah."

"Let's have it. It can't be that bad."

"I'll let you be the judge of that."

"Okay."

"Ian got an offer on the bar."

"An offer? Is it for sale? Did the guys put it on the market without telling me? Did you know?" Nikki's cheeks lost all their color.

"Jesus. Calm down or you'll go into labor right here and Stacy will kill me. No. Ian got an offer, but the bar isn't for sale. He wanted to let the guys know, that's all."

Nikki nodded. "That doesn't sound terrible. Dane had a problem with it?"

"Jerry Overland made the offer."

"Who's that?"

"Liz's husband. You said he's in development. He owns the mall."

"Oh. *Oh*. I guess Dane didn't like that."

"No."

"Is he okay?"

"I want to say yes, but I don't think so, Nik."

A large group of people came into the store, laughing and chatting about the marathon.

"I better get back to work. Thanks for telling me."

"No problem. I hope you're going home soon. I hurt just looking at you standing there."

"I feel okay, but someone comes in at one and I can leave then. It's finals week at the university, and some of the part-timers' schedules have been messed up because of that."

"Good, get some sleep."

"I will. Stacy keeps a journal." Nikki wrinkled her nose.

"You're a saint, that's all I can say."

Alyssa let herself out, running her hand along a new pair of running shoes.

Pregnancy was hard enough to go through for her own baby; she'd never do it for someone else.

Taking advantage of Sadie babysitting Drew, Alyssa went home for a quick nap. She had a feeling Brett would keep her up . . . all night.

# NIKKI

After a cool shower, Nikki Montgomery rubbed shea butter into the tight skin of her belly. She liked the feel of the babies moving under her hands.

No one understood why she would carry babies for her sister.

Stacy kept a brave face for everyone but her. Only she knew how much Stacy yearned for children of her own. After so many rounds of IVF, they couldn't afford to hire a surrogate, and even if they could, with her parents help, Jack wasn't on board with a stranger carrying his children.

When she and Stacy broached the subject with him, he agreed almost immediately. Stacy and Nikki shared blood, but more importantly, he knew Nikki lived a healthy life-style. She ran, ate well.

Dane had been the only hitch in the plan. It took a lot of convincing to get him to agree to the idea the first child she would carry wouldn't be theirs. She tried to explain the timing worked out better for them. Brett worked all the time. She didn't know how Alyssa battled with postpartum depression, got enough sleep, took care of her episiotomy stitches, and breastfed Drew by herself.

She tried to help when she could, but at the beginning Alyssa had a hard time letting her hold Drew, much less leaving him with her to sleep or go to the salon to get her hair done.

Something in Alyssa changed after Stacy and Jack's embryos took. Maybe Alyssa was able to look at her as a mother, but whatever it had been, Nikki took care of Drew a lot after that. She still babysat the little guy as much as she could giving Alyssa time to write, but mustering up the energy to run around after a toddler became harder and harder. Sadie, on the other hand, was a much better choice these days.

After letting the lotion soak into her skin and dressing in a maternity tank top and a matching pair of shorts, she sent Stacy her daily email. Her sister was a bit over the top when it came to micromanaging her day—emails, video chats, and phone calls all to make sure she was doing what she was supposed to be—but her sister wanted everything to go perfectly. Besides the fatigue that weighed on her no matter how many hours she slept, things were going well.

The twins were perfect.

Her doctor said this was a textbook case if she ever saw one.

Nikki was putting together a late dinner when Dane came home, and his foul mood made her skin clammy.

He still saw his therapist twice a month and still drank half the alcohol he used to before she ran out on him. She'd known what she was signing up for when she married him. The relationship with his parents had still been rocky, Liz hadn't faded into the background, and his relationship with Holly had still bothered her.

They were happy, but Dane's past wouldn't leave him alone, and he was always searching, always looking for something to blame her for. Something to accuse her of.

He'd deny it, if she ever told him that's how she felt.

She thought she could handle it, and for a long time she had.

Then the opportunity to help Stacy materialized, and she treaded lightly whenever the subject came up. Which it did, frequently, but she couldn't expect any less looking the way she did.

Now the offer on The Finish Line.

If Alyssa said he hadn't taken the news well, then he hadn't. She wasn't one to exaggerate.

Dane slammed the door and she jumped, cutting her hand with the knife she was using to slice tomatoes for salads.

"Crap." She shoved her finger into her mouth.

Dane dropped his keys onto the counter. "What happened?"

"I cut myself," she mumbled.

"Be careful." He pulled at her hand and examined the cut. It oozed blood. "You should wash it off."

"Ok—"

He yanked her hand under the faucet and turned on the stream.

"Ouch." She tried to pull her hand away. "You're hurting me."

Letting go he said, "Sorry. I'll get you a bandage."

"Thanks." Nikki pushed a paper towel to the cut and leaned against the counter.

Shaking the box, he came back into the kitchen and holding her hand, wrapped the bandage around her finger. "How's that?"

"Fine."

"I need to change."

He stomped toward the bedroom, his shoulders set in a rigid line.

She wanted to talk to him but she'd learned pushing him had the opposite affect she wanted, and they ate in silence, sitting at the small kitchen table. When she finished the last bite of lettuce, she said, "It's not a big deal, you know. You don't have to sell the bar."

Dane scoffed. "We probably will since Brett doesn't want to be a part of it anymore."

She dropped her fork. "Really? Alyssa didn't say anything when she came in to see me at the store. Can you and Ian run it alone?"

"I'll do what I have to do. I'm not selling to that asshole."

"You don't mean Ian?"

"Liz's husband. That fucker isn't getting his hands on something I worked so hard to build."

"Dane. That isn't necessary."

"What? Me calling him a fucker? It's not a coincidence he wants my bar."

"No, it's not. He buys successful businesses. You made The Finish Line a hot spot. Why wouldn't he want it?"

"Liz put him up to it because she doesn't want me to have anything."

He crossed his arms over his chest and stared sullenly at the table.

She tried to control her temper. Suppressing a groan, she stood and placed their bowls in the sink. "Not everything is about you. I'm going to bed."

"Do you feel okay?"

"What do you care?"

Dane let her go.

She waited for him to come into the bedroom to talk, but he never did.

# IAN

Ian dragged himself home after closing the bar. They could hire a manager, but it seemed an unnecessary expense when the three of them had shared the opening and closing duties up until now.

They did a lot on their own, made do with a minimal wait staff, and worked with a back-up bartender. Ian even helped Bobbi in the kitchen once or twice when one of her assistants had called in sick.

They all knew how to run the dishwasher.

After a year in business they had things down the way they wanted, but he had to admit it took a lot out of him, too.

A dim light lit up the living room, and Marta sat in a padded glider, feeding Hannah.

"Hey. What's up?"

"Giving Sadie a break. She watched Drew and Shyla for most of the day."

"She's a good girl."

"Who?"

"Sadie. She's come a long way. I'm proud of her."

Marta yawned. "She's a big help, that's for sure."

"She loves you, and she does it because you ask."

"She's a natural mother, but she tries to act tough and hide it. Drew adores her. That helps Alyssa feel better about leaving him here."

"She and Brett are having sex again," he said.

She laughed quietly. "And you know this how?"

Ian sat on the couch. Hannah sucked the bottle almost dry. She and Shyla looked so much alike when they were out in public people thought they were sisters.

"Dane was teasing them at the meeting. You didn't hear?"

"No, I must have been on the phone. That's good, though."

"You don't care," he asked, pressing her. They'd come a long way, he and Marta, but her history with Brett might always leave a sour taste in his mouth.

"Why would I care? Ian, don't start this."

"You didn't know Brett was tired of the bar? He didn't come over and pour his heart out?"

"I'm at marathon headquarters all day. When would I have time to talk to him? The race is next weekend."

"At headquarters, then. He didn't talk to you, tell you that he was fed up? Maybe ask for his job back?"

He wanted a fight. Wanted somewhere to shove his fear and uncertainty, but she knew him well. Too well to take the bait.

"Ian."

"What am I going to do? Brett wants out. Dane won't sell to Jerry Overland. I don't know if I want to run the bar without Brett, and I can't afford to buy him out. Not now."

"He knows what the bar brings in. He knows if he cuts out you won't be able to pay him yet. Maybe the money isn't as important as his time. You miss Shyla and Hannah just as much as Brett misses Drew. It's not hard to see his point of view. We talked about finding the time to marry, just like Brett said at the meeting. If he wants out, let him out. Under the stipulation you'll buy him out over a five-year period or something like that. He'll take it."

"Just let him go, just like that?" The idea nauseated him. They'd worked so hard, the three of them.

"You can't make him stay."

Marta pulled the empty bottle out of Hannah's mouth. The baby blinked her sleepy eyes open and raised her arms for Ian to take her.

He gathered her warm body to his chest and the little girl fell back asleep with her head on his shoulder.

This is what mattered.

Family.

The love Marta had for him. Her patience, her understanding when he wanted to take punches at her and the entire world.

He pressed a kiss to the top of his niece's head. "I'm sorry."

She tucked herself into his side and kissed his cheek. "We found a rhythm and now Brett's upsetting that. It made you scared and probably a little pissed, but it's not the end of the world. I love you."

Gripping the back of her neck, Ian pulled her in for a kiss. She steadied his shaky world. "I'm sorry. I was a prick. I love you, too."

"Talk to Brett. Tell him you understand because it's the truth. Then talk to Dane and figure out what his thoughts are. He's pissed and feels like he's living in Liz's shadow, but Ian? The offer was really that generous?"

"You want to think about selling The Finish Line?"

"I think we should consider it. Did Jerry give you a deadline?"

"No."

"Then *think* about it. If the offer is too good to pass up, then maybe you shouldn't."

"I love that bar."

"Yeah, me too. But change doesn't always have to be bad. Come on, let's go to bed."

Change didn't have to be bad.

Marta had played the cards she'd been dealt, turning into a mother for Shyla, even a surrogate mother to Sadie and Hannah. She'd gone from career woman to family woman in the space of a few months. Without complaint.

If she could change life directions with a smile on her face, then he could too, because what was important was their love for each other. Nothing else mattered, and in his panic, he'd forgotten that.

"I'm going to sit with Hannah for a few more minutes."

"Okay." She ran her hand over the back of Hannah's head.

Instead of heading upstairs, she shuffled into the kitchen. Five minutes later she set a mug of coffee on the table.

"Thank you."

"You're welcome. Ian?"

"Yeah?"

"There's nothing between me and Brett."

Shame burned his cheeks. "I know."

"Then please stop throwing my relationship with him in my face when we have a disagreement. We should be done with that by now."

"I'd get over it faster if I didn't have to see him all the time."

"Then maybe he's doing you a favor. Don't be long."

"I won't."

It hurt his heart when she carefully navigated the stairs, favoring the ankle she'd broken. It still gave her a bit of trouble, and she held the rail as she limped up the stairs.

He sat with Hannah until he couldn't keep his eyes open another minute. After settling her in her crib, he crawled into bed where Marta waited.

They would work out what would happen with The Finish Line.

No matter what, they were together, and everything would work out for the best.

# MARTA

M arta sat behind her desk at marathon headquarters. Sadie had finals to take, and she'd dropped the girls at daycare on her way to work. Like any mother, she hated trusting someone else to take care of the babies she thought of as her children, but Shyla ran away giggling, already anticipating a day with friends. Hannah had latched on to one of the workers, and barely blinked when Marta waved and made a quick getaway like the parenting magazines recommended instead of drawing out a goodbye and risking tears.

Ian had still been sleeping when she left with the girls strapped into the backseat of the minivan they'd purchased last year.

He only brought up Brett when he was stressed out or feeling particularly insecure.

Even though she understood his reason for his default reaction, she wished he'd stop doing it. It hurt her and after a year and a half he should have gotten over it by now.

But if Dane was still stuck on what Liz had done to him, maybe moving on wouldn't be so easy for Ian, either.

She didn't have any answers.

All she could do was understand where he was coming from and remind him she wasn't going anywhere. With as many times as she'd run out on him, that was on her and it was her responsibility to hang in there and fix it.

They needed to get married. It would help both of them to say vows and make promises.

It hadn't helped Dane, though. Well, marrying had turned him around, but Nikki carrying her sister's babies twisted him up. How Dane was handling that needed to be a worry for another day.

Marta got to work making phone calls, ensuring deliveries, confirming the band and their start time for the finish line party. Next year she'd see about the bar catering the after-party.

It would be good business and good marketing. Or maybe host a private dinner for the donors. She would talk to Ian and Dane about it.

Crap. If they didn't sell the bar.

No wonder everyone felt on edge. Just when things were settling down, life decided to stick a foot out and make them fall flat on their faces.

She was close to wrapping up her day and scooting out of headquarters when her cell phone rang. The number didn't look familiar, but she answered anyway.

"Hello. Marta speaking."

"Hello, Marta. I'm glad I caught you. This is Babbs Dresden with the Lady Slipper in Springfield. How are you doing?"

She slipped down the narrow hallway and closed the door to a private office Brett had used to make the more important phone calls. Like Brett, she did most of the marathon business in the main room with the other volunteers. They were a family and they worked together, but Marta felt this call would take more of a personal bend.

"Good. The marathon in Tower City is next weekend, so things are busy around here. And you?"

Babbs ignored the question. "And your ankle?"

Marta didn't hide the truth. "It didn't heal as well as my surgeon hoped, and I don't run anymore. What can I do for you, Ms. Dresden?"

"Has your attorney been in contact with you?"

"My attorney?"

"You *did* sue Gregory Spaulding for damages, didn't you?"

It had been so long ago Marta forgot all about it. "I guess I did."

"I heard from our attorney, and we won our suit against him and Libbie Layne's stepsister. For a moment it appeared as if we were going to be held responsible for her being on our course. But my attorney submitted race footage to show how chaotic the course is and how easy it would be for someone who doesn't belong to blend in."

Marta had never blamed any part of the Lady Slipper for her injury. Race day was usually full of commotion, and what Babbs said was true. Anyone could be on the course. The Boston Marathon bombing was proof of that.

"I'm glad the race isn't taking any of the blame for my injury. I never blamed you or the race. Things happen. Runners hurt themselves without any help. That could have been me."

She forced a smile, hoping Babbs would hear the sincerity in her voice and hang up. She wanted to pick up her girls. Maybe she'd take everyone to The Finish Line for dinner. Shyla always got a kick out of Ian bringing her food to their table.

"You should call your attorney. Ask him for the details."

"Thank you. I will."

She waited for Babbs to say her goodbyes but the older woman hesitated.

"This has been hard on me. The investigation, the scandal. We may have escaped being held accountable but that doesn't take your injury away, and it's a regret I've lived with since the second you fell."

"You don't have to feel that way," she said touched she'd been on Babbs's mind all this time.

"That's kind of you to say, but the race doesn't have the same feel to me as it's had in the past, and the October's Lady Slipper will be my last."

"I'm sorry to hear that."

"I'm sorry, too, but it's time for me to retire. Marta, what are your plans? Are you happy directing that tiny marathon after organizing all those prestigious retreats?"

"I've never thought about it. I'm more about my family these days. I'm engaged and in the process of adopting his daughter. Why?"

Babbs sounded older than her years when she said, "I'm offering you my position. I'd take the next year to ease you in, but you wouldn't need me for more than that. You have a good head on your shoulders. I would feel good leaving the Slipper in your hands."

"This is . . . unexpected."

"Not for me. I've been considering it for a while now. Not to mention, it would be good PR for the race. You dropped off the face of the earth, Marta. Speculation is rampant you blame the race for your career being destroyed."

She propped her feet on the desk. "I hadn't realized."

"Well, I heard you turned down the coaching position

at the school, and Spaulding's position, too. Are you not committed to the running community anymore?"

"It's hard to feel part of a community doing what you can't. When I announced my retirement, this wasn't what I had in mind."

"Then perhaps you won't be interested in my offer after all."

"I didn't say that."

"You didn't have to. But, contact me after the marathon. If you can make the time, we could meet in person to talk about it."

"That sounds good, Ms. Dresden." She paused. "It's not that I dropped off the face of the earth. A wise man told me there's more to life than running. I've been finding just how true that is."

"I'm happy for you. Keep in touch. And good luck to you and your race participants."

"Thank you," she murmured, but Babbs had already hung up.

Out of curiosity, she touched base with her attorney. She contacted one because Ian had told her to, then she brushed it aside with personal issues. She agreed Spaulding should be held accountable for what he'd done to her, but she hadn't followed the case. She didn't know how involved Libbie Layne had been, or what happened to her stepsister.

She'd been too busy with Ian, with Sadie and Hannah, and with mothering Shyla.

On her way to the car she gave him a call.

"Miss Braddock, I've been meaning to get in touch, but you beat me to it. You heard about the verdict, then."

"Ah, no. I actually just spoke with Babbs Dresden. She let me know the case was resolved."

"Yes, and in your favor. We didn't want to go after the

school, but that's what happened. Gregory Spaulding was under the employ of the university and they should be held accountable."

Marta listened to the details as she drove to Shyla and Hannah's daycare center.

"Why didn't I need to testify?" she asked, pulling into the parking lot.

"We had the video of your accident, your statement, and the statement from your surgeon explaining the extent of your injury. You weren't needed as a witness."

"Oh."

"It's not so unusual. Gregory Spaulding didn't testify, either. His defense attorney thought it best, but in the end it didn't matter. There was too much evidence stacked against him for his side of the story to do any good."

When her attorney told her the sum the court awarded her, Marta slammed on the brakes.

"Did you add an extra zero by mistake?"

Her attorney laughed. "Eighteen months later you still suffer from mild pain and you can't run anymore. Because a man wanted his paramour in your position, he took away your livelihood. He'll plea down and be let out on time served and good behavior, but his academic career is over. I've heard his wife is filing for divorce, but Ms. Layne is sticking by him. It's kind of her—she's all he has left after this whole nightmare."

Marta parked and turned off the engine. "Thank you for doing that for me."

"It's what you paid me for, Miss Braddock. I'll reach out when I hear more. Take care."

"Have a nice evening."

That kind of money could change things for her and

Ian. They'd be able to afford a nice wedding and take the girls on vacation to celebrate.

Ian could buy out Brett's share of The Finish Line.

There were possibilities within reach.

When she went inside, Shyla launched herself into her arms and Marta buried her face in the little girl's hair.

A daycare staff member handed Hannah to her, the toddler beaming, ready to go.

"Let's go home, sweeties."

She had lots of news to share.

## ALYSSA

Thinking it time to start moving, Alyssa texted Nikki and asked if she felt up for a walk, and Nikki met her on the path behind the loft. The trails held a lot of memories for Alyssa. She'd put in several weeks of training with Brett for the runner's manual through the park. It's where he'd broken her heart. And where she'd broken his.

She pushed Drew in his stroller, and at a snail's pace, they started out.

"How are you feeling?" she asked.

Nikki looked more tired recently, and with every day that passed, her belly grew bigger and bigger.

"Tired. Sore. They move around a lot and I don't get much sleep. I need to talk to Dane about cutting my hours at the store. He won't like it, but I can't help it. It's hard to stay on my feet for so long. I'll be glad when the marathon is over."

"I hope Brett's announcement didn't cause problems."

Nikki scowled. "Of course it did. The bar's been open for barely a year and he already wants out. I get it, but their schedules won't always be like that. Dane knows more about opening a business, I guess." Her voice squeaked.

"I'm sorry."

"It's not your fault. It's not even Brett's. When I married Dane, I knew he had some baggage and I thought we could work through it. Then he blows up and accuses Liz of gunning for him. We've had disagreements, but we had our first fight over Jerry Overland. It's stupid."

Alyssa pushed Drew and took a deep breath of spring air. She hadn't spent enough time outside. The sun lifted her spirits and Drew loved looking around. Hunter required more than what she'd been giving him, too. The dog sniffed the grass, his ears perking up as a flock of birds scattered from a tree, flying into the blue sky.

After a rocky year, things were starting to smooth out. It wasn't fair things were going better for her, and now Nikki was miserable.

"They can't sell if they aren't all in," Alyssa said.

"They could sell. Two against one. Dane can't buy them both out. If Brett and Ian vote to take Jerry's offer, then Dane would have no choice but to go along. I wish this had never happened."

"If it wouldn't have been this, it would have been something else. Dane has always had an edge to him, Nik. Maybe you wore it down, but it didn't go away."

"It's the babies. He hates that I'm doing this for Stacy. He's an only child and he doesn't understand what it's like to see your sibling hurting. I'll never forget the joy on Stacy's face when I told her I would surrogate. She couldn't stop crying. I told Dane I wish I would have done it sooner. Then it wouldn't have caused problems."

"What did he say?"

"That I was too busy chasing rich guys to think of it."

"Oh, honey. That doesn't sound like him."

"I know. That's why I can't understand it. I want to go stay with Stacy until the babies are ready. But running didn't help last time, and it won't help now."

"Is there anything I can do?"

Nikki smiled, blinking back tears. "No, but thanks. I'm hoping things will go back to normal after the babies are born. But this Jerry Overland crap will have to come first. I doubt he'll give the guys too much longer to decide."

They finished their walk in silence, Hunter's nails scraping the cement, Drew cooing at the clouds, eventually falling asleep.

They parted ways when they finished the loop. She would ask Brett to talk to Dane.

Anything could help.

# BRETT

"That won't help. And the last person he wants to talk to is me."

"But Nikki's miserable."

Brett shook his head and set the table. Drew slammed a toy on his highchair tray and let out a yell of happiness.

"Someone's in a good mood."

"I took him out earlier. The fresh air did him some good."

"And you, too." He pulled her into his arms. "You scared me the other night."

"When?" His shirt muffled her voice.

"When I thought you were telling me to move out."

She lifted her head. "I live here, too, you know. I know you haven't been happy."

"There must be something in the water. I can talk to Dane, but it won't do any good. He should be talking to the therapist he loves so much. I thought Nikki got him over Liz."

"I thought so, too."

He stirred the gravy that would go on Drew's favorite

mashed potatoes. At one year old, he still liked a bottle, but he liked small amounts of solid food, too. Mashed potatoes, a little ice cream, though if Alyssa caught him, she'd bitch him out with a smile on her face.

He'd caught her sneaking him tastes of her Greek yogurt, and he didn't feel too guilty.

Brett sat at the table with his little family. He wanted more of this, and he wouldn't get it as a third of The Finish Line. No matter how guilty he felt, no matter how many problems he caused, Alyssa and Drew were his first priority, and he wouldn't regret speaking his mind.

He wanted to give his son everything he never had.

After dinner, he gave Drew a bath and fastened a clean diaper to his little butt. He knew Alyssa had been worried he wouldn't take to being a father, not after all the shit he gave her while they were dating—though that's not what she'd call their daily runs—but he'd never had a problem loving the little boy who had her dark hair and his eyes.

He never tired of leaning in for a wet kiss or reading bedtime stories until his voice grew hoarse. The Finish Line took up too much time. He couldn't wait to get rid of his share.

In the nursery, Drew snuggled on his chest, and Brett read him bedtime stories while Alyssa carved out a couple of hours of writing time.

His watch said ten-thirty when Drew finally dropped off to sleep. He took the stairs to the loft.

Alyssa sat in front of her computer, a bowl of nuts at her elbow, a pencil in her mouth, her fingers flying across the keys.

"Good scene?"

"They all are," she mumbled. "He go down okay?"

"Yeah. Hey, I'll go talk to Dane if that's what you really want."

Alyssa turned away from the monitor. "Is it his turn to work?" she asked around the pencil clenched between her teeth.

"He's there with Ian. I should be able to grab him for a few minutes. You're right. We've been friends for a long time. Maybe he'll spill his guts."

She pulled the pencil from her mouth. "I hope so. I hate how upset Nikki was this afternoon. She said when it comes to selling the place it will be you and Ian against Dane. Did Ian tell you what he wanted?"

"No. But Ian misses Shyla just as much as I miss Drew. I would be surprised if he didn't feel the same way I do."

"But if you just hang in there a little bit longer . . . she seems to think it will all slow down."

"The only way it will slow down is if we hire more help. What's the point of that when we're capable of doing all the work?"

Brett sat on the edge of the rocking recliner. "It's the same with Dane's store. He ran it alone for a long time because he could. Because he had to. When we finally make a profit, we're going to use it to hire someone? There's not a lot of sense in that when we could pocket it."

"What will Jerry Overland do with it then?"

"It'll cost him to buy us out and to staff it. But he's thinking long term, and I'm not willing to do that. Maybe in five years it would make sense to hire more staff, but how much of Drew's life would I miss if we waited that long? And we might want to have another baby before then."

Her mouth fell open. "You want more kids?"

Brett stood and paced. He hadn't meant to say that. Her pregnancy and delivery hadn't been easy and watching her go through it had torn him up. He'd felt so helpless watching her day after day, taking it hour by uncomfortable hour until Drew's birth.

It had scared the fuck out of him when Drew came out, purple, the cord wrapped around his neck. Couldn't see through the tears as they stitched up Alyssa's episiotomy and the nurses worked on Drew, giving him oxygen, coaxing him to breathe.

When Drew's delivery should have been the happiest day of his life, it had been the most terrifying.

"I grew up an only child, and I always wondered if how my parents treated me would have somehow not hurt so much if I would have had someone to go through it with. I would love for Drew to have a brother or a sister. He loves Hannah and Shyla. If you were willing, and if it was safe."

She sniffled, wiping the tears from her face. "I always thought pressing you to have Drew was a mistake."

Brett leaned his hip against her desk and brushed her hair away from her cheek. "I was fucking scared when you told me you were pregnant. Even though we planned it, I was fucking scared. Because of the way I grew up. Because of Marta. But you gave me my life when Drew was born. You gave me a future. Drew wasn't a mistake. I love that little kid more than I could ever explain to anyone."

She blew out a breath. "Wow. You've given me a lot to think about. The only aunts and uncles Drew will have will be honorary. I always felt kind of bad about that."

"I don't think we could ask for better." Dane and Nikki, Ian and Marta. He'd never find people he trusted more to take his little boy if anything ever happened to him and Alyssa.

"You're right. We couldn't. And Dane is having a tough time. You should go talk to him."

"I'll try not to be out too late. You know, I used to rebel against a nine to five, but from where I'm sitting right now, it's looking pretty good."

She squeezed his hand. "Be careful."

"I will. Going to bed soon?"

"Maybe after this scene."

He pressed a kiss to her forehead. "Good. Don't stay up too late."

After poking his head into the nursery and making sure Drew was still sound asleep, Brett drove to The Finish Line.

Cars filled the parking lot and people packed the benches waiting for a table or space to free up at the bar.

Through one of the large picture windows, he could see Ian mixing drinks. A group of young women were giggling while they sipped on cocktails ogling him. He went with the flow, grinned at the jokes, popped the gum that always seemed to be in his mouth. Every night he made a mint in tips.

Brett could be just as charming, but slowly, before he'd begun to put a name to it, the discontentment of having to spend so much time at the bar started to seep into the way he treated the customers. Not a lot, but a little. And that was when he knew he had to get out. When he stopped having fun. If he was going to spend sixty hours a week of his time somewhere, he better damn well enjoy it.

Brett fought his way past the hostess podium. He should be at home snuggling his fiancée, maybe making love since they discovered it wouldn't hurt her. Sleeping because tomorrow would be a long day and his turn to close this place.

Fighting the crowd, he good-naturedly waved off patrons who wanted him to stop and chat.

Ian raised his eyebrows when he approached the bar. "Want a drink?"

"No. I came to talk to Dane. Is he around?"

"You have good timing," Ian said, pulling a beer from a tap, a white bar towel slung over his shoulder. "He's out back taking a break."

"Thanks."

Brett saluted Bobbi as he walked through the kitchen to reach the rear door. She flew around putting together burger baskets, chicken strip meals, and dishing up a spicy macaroni and cheese entrée that quickly became The Finish Line's signature dish.

The traffic humming along the main strip buzzed in his ears, and he scanned the lot for Dane. They'd set up a picnic table for the staff who wanted a place to get off their feet for a bit while getting some fresh air, and they'd moved the dumpster as far away from the building as possible. In the summer months it kept the smell and bugs away from the break area. Bobbi set out some potted plants, though the bright colors didn't add much to the concrete jungle.

Tonight the bluish-white light wavered from the street-lights and they cast Dane's shadow long and narrow as he paced several feet from the building.

He held a phone to his ear.

"Dane," Brett said, taking a few steps toward him.

He jerked up his head, and if Brett didn't know better, a look of panic flashed across his friend's face.

"I need to go. No, everything is fine. I'll call you tomorrow. Thanks for talking to me. Goodnight." Dane shoved his phone into his back pocket. "What are you doing here? If you don't want to be here when you have to be, why are you here on your day off?"

"I came by to talk to you."

The corner of Dane's mouth turned down. "And it couldn't wait?"

"We're all a little worried about you, that's all."

"I'm fine."

"Are you? Because Nikki told Alyssa—"

"It's none of your business what's going on between Nik and me. It's private and has nothing to do with you."

"If you're unhappy with me because I want out, don't take it out on her."

"You do whatever the fuck you want. You always have."

"That's not true."

"It's not? You want to write a book, you write a book whether Alyssa wants to help you or not. You don't want to direct the marathon anymore, you get out, and Marta conveniently takes your place. You don't want to help run the bar anymore, and all of a sudden someone wants to take it off our hands. Did you approach Overland and tell him we'd sell if we had an offer?"

Brett took a step back. "Is that what you think?"

"It isn't what I think, it's what I know." Dane pointed to the building. "We had a good business. A solid business. We're already in the black and you want to ruin it. We can't run this place without you, and Ian and I would need years to buy you out. Overland called to press us for an answer, and Ian accepted. Didn't bother to ask if I was okay with it. It's done."

The inside of Brett's mouth felt grainy and dry. Because he wanted more time with Alyssa and his son, he'd destroyed the best friendship he ever had. Dane had stuck by him when his parents wanted nothing to do with him. They'd celebrated holidays together, ran together, put on the best damned marathon the city had ever seen together, and all that history was gone.

"I'm sorry."

"No, you're not. You got your way. *Again*. Go home. I have work to do."

Dane slammed into the building leaving him alone in the parking lot.

He hadn't been that selfish, had he? To want more time with his family? It hurt they hadn't sat down and talked about it, but that was stupid too. When he said he wanted out, he'd removed himself from any decisions Dane and Ian made concerning the business, and that included selling it.

He sank onto the picnic table's bench.

Ian pushed out of the back door, propped a foot on the bench next to him and rested his forearm on his knee.

"Dane told you I took Overland's offer."

"Yeah."

"It's not your fault."

"Dane seems to think so."

"He'll get over it. Once he sees the check for his share, he'll get over it. Things are changing, and he doesn't want to accept it. He's still stuck in the past, when we were single and didn't have kids. He wants that time back, and he's never going to get it back."

"I was thinking the same thing. When we would spend nights in your bar bullshitting and eating peanuts. No rugrats to rush home to, no fiancées to bitch at as for staying out late. Things were simpler then."

Ian shook his head. "Simpler, maybe. But not better. The past couple years have shaken me up just as much as they've shaken up Dane. My dad selling the bar and our apartments out from under us, my sister's pregnancy. Marta gave me a run for my money. I never knew from one day to the next if she was really going to stay, or if I was going to wake up one morning and she'd be gone, leaving a note on the table and three broken hearts behind her. I never said anything to Dane, and maybe I should have, but I agree with you. Marta and I put our wedding on hold, same as you and Alyssa. We proved we could build a business from scratch, make it profitable. Maybe now it's time to move on."

"I'm worried about him."

Ian snapped the gum between his teeth. "He's a grown-ass man. He's got a wife, and he almost fucked that up, too. If Nikki can't keep him in line, no one can. Sometimes you gotta grow the fuck up. Pissing and moaning about who bought the bar. Pissing and moaning because his wife is a surrogate for her sister. What he's got going on now doesn't have anything to do with us."

Brett bit the inside of his cheek. "I still feel responsible."

"No one's responsible for Dane but Dane. If he's having a tough time accepting things the way they are, that's not on you."

"When I came out here, he was talking to someone. It wasn't Nikki."

Ian scoffed. "Don't step in that pile of shit; you'll never get it off your shoe. Nikki isn't blind and she can take care of herself. She's proven that. If Dane's decided to step out, then it's probably better for all involved the babies in her belly don't belong to them."

"You think Dane would cheat on Nikki?" Brett tried to picture it, but he couldn't. He remembered peeling Dane off the floor of Ian's bar when Dane had accused her of cheating on him with her ex, Eric. Dane had been a nervous mess waiting for Nikki to talk to him so he could apologize. Dane hadn't gone through all that only to cheat on her a year later.

"I think Dane doesn't know what he wants right now. He's confused, and he's hurt. Nikki should be his safe place, but everyone knows he resents her carrying Stacy's babies. That's between them and I don't have any opinions on that at all. I need to get back inside. Overland's coming by tomorrow, just so you know. Give him the books, a tour, anything he wants to look at."

"Right."

Ian slapped him on the shoulder before stepping inside the building to finish his shift, music and laughter escaping in a loud burst when he opened the door.

Brett sat at the picnic table as cars crowded the road.

Things were changing, and he would never know if letting go of The Finish Line was a mistake he would later come to regret. All he could do now was shake it off.

What was done was done.

# IAN

Ian woke to an empty house.

Though he was grateful for the undisturbed hours of sleep, it let him down, too. No sloppy kisses from Shyla to wake him up, no scent of coffee and pancakes to make his stomach grumble. No Hannah in the kitchen slamming toys on her highchair tray as she waited for Sadie to make her a bowl of infant oatmeal.

Sadie needed to go to campus to speak to her advisor about fall semester classes, and Marta would be at race headquarters doing her thing while the girls were at daycare.

He had the day free, and he started by grabbing a cup of coffee from the carafe Marta kept heated for him. After sipping a mug and scanning the newspaper, he started on chores.

Laundry, cleaning the bathrooms, vacuuming.

It took him a couple of hours to set the house to rights and pull out enough chicken from the freezer to feed his family of five. When the toys were put away and the towels folded, he took a shower and stopped at The Finish Line to pick up an order.

He didn't want to get into it with Dane, and he'd said his piece to Brett last night.

Ian parked in the back and snuck into the kitchen. Bobbi's assistant handed him a to-go bag and he shot her a smile before slinking out to his car, hopefully undetected.

Marta sat at her desk talking on the phone when he stepped into marathon headquarters, and she brightened when she saw him. "Sounds good. Thanks. Bye." She hung up. "What are you doing here?"

"I thought I'd bring my beautiful fiancée lunch. Do you have a problem with that?"

She grinned. "Nope, as long as that beautiful fiancée is me."

"Then it's your lucky day."

"Come into the back. Too noisy in here."

Ian followed her down the little hallway, past a break room where three runners sat arguing. They quieted when Marta passed by and lowered their eyes.

"What's that about?" he asked, closing the door to a small office with a desk.

"They feel bad I can't run anymore. It's like shooting a Kentucky Derby winner when he breaks a leg. There's a . . . tragedy about it, I guess. I used to let it bother me, but now I just take it for the sympathy it is."

"Do you miss it?" Ian asked, unpacking the chicken strips she liked, and a thick, greasy, bacon cheeseburger for himself.

Marta pushed a chair closer to his and pulled two bottles of water out of a little cooler. "Running? I thought I would. Apart from what I kept telling myself I gave up to keep doing it." She ran a finger along his clean-shaven cheek, and he caught her hand and kissed her palm. "But I think of all I received in return, and I don't. Running brought me to you. I came back to Minnesota because of the sport, but it's gone and I'm still here."

Ian blinked and hoped she didn't see the tears making his vision waver. That was probably the most honest thing she'd ever told him about her still being in Minnesota. Not anything about her baby, not really, nothing about Brett. Nothing about regret or resentment.

Only a quiet resolve to accept how things were, and to be happy with what she had.

She stepped between his legs and cradled his face between her hands.

Shit. She'd seen his emotion after all. He'd never been good at keeping things from her.

"Are you okay?" she asked.

"Yeah. Sometimes I feel . . ."

"Like this is too good to be true?"

"Something like that."

Marta took her seat and peeled the waxed paper away from her chicken strips. "I feel like that too, when Shyla calls me Mama. Or when you look at me like you love me so much you can't speak. I know what little I brought to the table, and you still wanted me."

"I didn't want anything more than you."

"It took me a long time to believe that."

They ate in silence for a moment, and Ian tried to think of the best way to tell her his news.

"I didn't get to see you last night or this morning, and I have some news," Marta said.

"Oh?" He tried not to sound like she threw him a life vest.

"Yeah. Babbs Dresden called me yesterday. She's retiring and wants me to take over."

"She wants you to direct the Lady Slipper? In Springfield?"

"Yeah."

"What did you tell her?"

"That I'd need to think about it, and talk to you, of course. I don't know, Ian. We would have to move, and I . . . it would be difficult for me to want to direct a race I can't run. The Tower City Marathon is different somehow. Brett and Dane are my friends, and I stepped in because there wasn't anyone else."

She pushed her basket away and wiped her fingers on a napkin that came with their meals.

Ian took the plunge and blurted, "We sold the bar yesterday."

Her startled eyes flew to his. "God. I'm sorry."

"Are you mad I didn't talk to you about it?"

She shook her head. "Brett made a mess of things, didn't he?"

"It wasn't him. I know how he feels. I love the bar, but I love you more. This year, we should have been married. We should have been, I don't know." He rested his elbow on the desk and balled his napkin in his hand. "I don't feel as terrible as Brett does. I had time with Shyla before we bought The Finish Line, but I understood his point. I understand Dane's, too. We put all this work in just to throw it away? Well, Brett didn't want to keep it, and Dane didn't want to run it without him. Sale will go through in a couple of days."

"We'll always be on the outside."

"Is that what you think that is?"

Marta jerked a shoulder. "Maybe. I don't know. Brett

getting out was more important in the end than Jerry Overland buying it, and Dane had pretty strong feelings about
that."

"I guess so." It hadn't occurred to him to feel slighted
Dane didn't want to keep the bar running without Brett. "It
was a money thing too, though."

"Brett doesn't need the cash. He could have waited for
his share. I'm sorry. I don't mean to make it sound like Dane
would have done anything else than run The Finish Line
with you."

"No, I get it. They were always better friends. Makes
me feel better Dane and I didn't give it a go. It might not
have turned out so well, and we wouldn't have had the offer
to fall back on."

"Yeah."

"Well, this frees us up, anyway. We can move to Springfield if you want to give the Lady Slipper a go."

She blinked. "You'd move for me?"

He tossed the crumpled napkin at her. "Sure. We don't
have ties to this place, unless Trent's parents give Sadie a
hard time about moving. They spend more time with
Hannah than I thought they would, but Trent hasn't
wanted anything to do with her. Unless they sue Sadie for
partial custody—which we would fight—she's free to do as
she likes."

"But you grew up here."

"And there's nothing left. My parents are gone, and my
relationship with you is more important than my friendships with Brett and Dane. If you want to direct the Lady
Slipper, I'll support you. A change of scenery might be good
for Sadie. She doesn't have friends her age and she should
still have a little social life. Maybe meet some younger

mothers like herself and organize some playdates for Hannah."

"But our beautiful house." She sucked in a breath. "I talked to my attorney yesterday. Babbs recommended I call him. The case is closed, and they awarded me a lot of money."

She told him a figure that made him choke. "Are you serious?"

"Yeah. Less attorney fees, I'm assuming, but yeah. We can pay off the house, take the girls on vacation. Get married. All the things we've wanted to do."

He laughed. "Christ, Marta. If you would have told me that before . . . that's enough to buy both Dane *and* Brett out of their shares of The Finish Line and then some."

"Do you want to do that? Can you get out of your deal with Overland?"

"No, I don't. That's your money. Put it away. A nest egg never hurts."

She settled onto his lap, and he wrapped his arms around her.

"I don't think I want to direct the Lady Slipper. Babbs said it would be closure for the race, but I don't care."

With his hand to the back of her head, he pressed a kiss to her lips. "You don't want to do this anymore, do you, sweetheart?"

"No. I thought I could still enjoy it, but when my ankle didn't heal, I guess I lost my joy in the sport."

"Running has been a big part of your life, and sometimes it's hard to turn a corner—"

Trying not to smile, she slapped his arm.

Laughing, he said, "Figuratively speaking. I thought The Finish Line would be a part of our lives forever. I pictured Shyla waitressing there, but we barely got it off the ground. I guess we'll have to revisit and revise."

Marta stood and threw their trash into the paper bag. "Let's get out of here. I know a better place to revisit and revise."

He ran a finger up her arm, and she shivered. "Does this place serve dessert?"

"Sure does. On the menu it's called Afternoon Delight. Whipped cream included."

"Hmm. I like this place already."

He pulled her in for a kiss and she ran her hand down the fly of his jeans.

"Then hurry up."

Ian held the door open for her and shut the light out behind them.

In the parking lot, he swept her in his arms and twirled her around.

She gasped, her arms tightening around his neck.

Maybe he and Marta didn't know what they would do professionally, but the fact they were on the same page emotionally was more important to him.

He wished Dane would straighten out his personal life too, before he did something he'd regret.

# DANE

Dane sat in his truck outside the Tower City Shopping Center. This was a bad idea, but he couldn't stop himself from going into the most prestigious women's clothing store in the city. He couldn't stop himself from taking the escalator to the second floor or finding the suite of offices where the store's executives pushed paper.

A bubbly blonde receptionist pointed him in the right direction, though he already knew where to go.

He knocked on her door and clenched his jaw while he waited for her to answer.

The plaque fastened to the wood mocked him.

Elizabeth Overland.

"Come in."

The knob turned in his hand, and he stepped onto the plush carpeting of her corner office.

Liz sat behind a huge desk, the surface covered in fabric swatches.

"What are you doing here?" she asked, narrowing her eyes.

He'd always wondered what her new husband saw in her.

Her hair gleamed, and she dressed in the most up-to-date fashions. The rings she wore on one hand could have bought Brett's share of the bar, but even with all those things, her eyes were flat and hard and the corners of her mouth turned down in a permanent frown.

He'd dressed for work and felt more on her level than he usually did wearing his running clothes.

"Did you tell your husband to make an offer on The Finish Line?"

Liz scoffed. "Why would I do that?"

"Because the bar's successful. Because it's a hot spot. Because I'm a part of it."

"He doesn't ask for my input regarding his business decisions."

"Really? Maybe you only like to spend his money."

"I work. Obviously. It's none of your business if I want to drive a nice car and live in a pretty house. You found a woman who's happy with your piece of shit truck and the crappy little apartment you still live in. Why can't that be enough for you?"

"It is."

"No, it's not, or you wouldn't be here. Has she fallen out of love already?" Liz smirked.

"Nikki doesn't have anything to do with this. I want to know if you put your husband up to buying the bar to spite me."

"That would imply I care about you and I don't. As I said, Jerry conducts his own business. If he made an offer on your shitty bar, take it as a compliment and move on."

"I put a lot of work into that bar."

Liz stood from her webbed chair and rounded her desk.

She rested her ass against the edge and crossed her arms over her breasts.

"Then open another one. You have a head for business—your store is doing well, too."

Dane snapped his mouth shut. He'd never known Liz to give him any praise.

"Why did you marry me?" he asked.

"I was young and stupid. In a way, I was in love with you. You've always had a boyish charm, but you're content to float through life. You put in the hard work when it suits you and slack off the rest of the time. And all that fucking running. God, you can wear a suit, but Jesus Christ. Always going for a fucking run."

"At least you can say you loved me, because I sure as hell loved you."

"I'm sorry I wanted more."

"More than me."

"You changed."

"How can you say that? Throughout our whole marriage everything I did, I did for you. I breathed for you. I did everything you asked."

"And in the process turned into a doormat. You did everything I told you to do, and I lost all respect for you. Who wants to be with a man who won't speak up for himself?"

"You're unbelievable. All I did was try to make you happy, and you're twisting it into something pathetic."

"If the stiletto fits."

"I'm not going to listen to this." He turned to go. Like hell he'd listen to her warp his love into something spineless and meaningless.

"You don't think it's true?"

He turned around. "No, I don't."

She tossed her hair over her shoulder. "What about the bar then? Jerry said Ian took the deal. Why? If you love that bar so much?"

"Brett wanted out."

"Right. You and Ian couldn't *possibly* have run it without him. Did you tell Ian you wanted a partnership with him? No. You gave up. Gave in. Brett wanted out and you sat in the corner like a little kid, crying."

He stilled.

She was right.

He hadn't entertained the idea he and Ian could've run it alone. Brett said he wanted out, and he sulked, just like Liz accused him of. He never asked Ian if he wanted to run the bar without Brett. In his mind, it was the three of them or none of them.

He'd made Ian give up because he couldn't bend.

"You're right."

"And Nikki?"

Dane stiffened. "What about her?"

"She's carrying her sister's babies. I hear you're not too happy about that."

"Where do you hear this garbage?"

"I have my ear to the ground. But it's true, isn't it? I can see it on your face."

He shrugged. He wouldn't admit it bothered him. Nikki's surrogacy was between them and no one else.

"Why didn't you tell her no?"

"It was important to her that she do it for Stacy."

"You think her sister is more important than her marriage? You think if you would have told her you didn't want her to do it, she would have anyway?"

"It doesn't matter. It's done."

"That's what I'm trying to tell you. The night Jerry and

I ran into you downtown, she stood up to me and told me off in the five minutes we talked and that's more than you ever did the whole time we were married. You stood there, cowering, just like always. You didn't tell Nikki you didn't want her to surrogate. How is she supposed to know? You're going to teach her to walk all over you just the way you taught me. I lost all respect for you, and mark my words, so will Nikki. Then it will be her fault you're unhappy just like it was mine."

"I started the store without telling you."

Liz stepped across the office, her heels sinking into the carpet. She rested a hand on his bicep but he jerked away. "You did. By then it was too late, and I was too angry to be proud of you. If it's any consolation, we probably still would have gotten a divorce. You never seemed to have a goal, have a plan, and I'm more . . . direct. You and Nikki are a better match. That night downtown—the look in her eyes. She loves you. I hope you don't ruin it."

"Like you said, I'm a whiny little brat. I probably already have."

Dane stepped out of her office, and with his gaze fastened to the ground, walked out to his truck.

That was why Brett made him so angry. He reached out and took what he wanted. He said he wanted to write a book, and he found a way to make that happen. He didn't want to run the marathon anymore, and he stopped. He didn't put up with it year after year slowly letting it poison him until he hated the race. And himself.

And The Finish Line. He didn't want to run it anymore, so he took the steps he needed to take to get out.

He wasn't pissed at his friend for the choices he'd made. He was jealous Brett had the guts to make the choices at all.

If he'd wanted to run the bar with Ian, he should have

said something. Ian couldn't read his mind, and he sold the bar.

He needed to grow a pair.

Mulling over his conversation with Liz, he drove to The Finish Line. Seeing her hadn't been as bad as he thought it would be, and maybe he learned something, too. Because of his inability to speak his mind, The Finish Line no longer belong to them, and as he stood in the dining room, an emptiness weighed on him.

It didn't feel like theirs anymore, either.

"Hey," Ian said pushing into the dining room from the kitchen.

"Hey."

In silent agreement, they started the process of opening the restaurant. They put chairs onto the floor and checked the condiments on the tables.

"I saw Liz this morning," he said.

Ian shot him a look from across the room. "Yeah?"

"Yeah. She told me I needed to learn how to fucking speak my mind and not let people trample all over me." He drew in a breath. "Hey, if I would have told you I wanted to run this place without Brett, would you have been in?"

"Maybe, but you've always been tighter with Brett. I get it."

"I didn't want out because Brett did."

"You don't have to lie to make me feel better. Marta said we'll always be the outsiders, and it's okay. Dumping the bar was a good move. Time for something new."

Ian's observation made him feel like shit. "I should have said something."

"You don't get it. When you don't say anything, you say something. You made a choice by shoving the decision onto me. Don't put it on me because you feel bad about it."

"That's not what I'm doing."

"It's not? Because it's too late to talk about it when there's no going back. It's safe for you now. The choice has been made. You shake off responsibility like Hunter shakes water off his fur then wonder why you're unhappy all the time. Victim doesn't look good on you."

Ian ducked into the kitchen.

Dane served drinks and meals in a bar that no longer belonged to him. He'd tried to blame Ian for it, and Brett, but the deal Ian agreed to with Overland was all his fault. He could have stopped it and he didn't.

He needed to own that.

Take responsibility.

He and Ian worked their shifts barely speaking. Ian wasn't angry—that wasn't his way—but he sent Dane home early saying he'd notate the books and lock up.

Dane stood in the doorway of the office wanting to say something, but Ian brought up their bookkeeping software program and effectively shut him out.

After a mumbled "Goodnight" that Ian ignored, he dragged himself out to his truck.

Things weren't great at home, either. With their schedules overlapping, Nikki was sleeping when he came home and up and opening the store by the time he hauled himself out of bed, usually past noon on a night like this.

He missed her.

His phone rang as he settled behind the wheel.

Holly.

A wiggle of something he didn't want to name slithered through his stomach. "Hey. What are you doing up?"

She yawned, stretched, and moaned a little.

Before Nikki, that would have made him hard. But he was too tired, too . . . he wanted to say hurt, but people were throwing him lots of truths tonight and he didn't have the right to hurt.

Not when in the past few days he'd been the one doing it to other people. People he cared about.

People he loved.

"I woke up and couldn't fall back asleep. I thought you would be getting off work now if you wanted to continue our conversation."

A different night, maybe. He was also afraid of opening a door he couldn't close. When he'd run to Holly, he'd run to the wrong woman. If he couldn't talk to Nikki, he'd had no business marrying her.

Dane set the phone to speaker and placed it on his dusty dash. "Why did you stick it out with me for so long?"

"I think that's obvious. I was in love with you. I wanted to get married."

"You're beautiful and smart. You could have had any guy in the city. Why did you wait?"

"You're asking me why I was in love. How can anyone explain that? You're successful. Got a great bod from all that running. You're cute, and you had that fixer-upper, damaged way about you. I was starstruck when we met in that bar, and that night you came home with me and we made love, I was halfway there. I would have waited forever."

He drove through the city, the streets quiet at that time of morning. Fatigue settled in his bones. He'd made so many mistakes, some of them unfixable.

"You knew I didn't feel the same way."

"Hope and logic don't always go hand in hand," she said laughing, thick like smoke, drifting through the cab of his truck.

"I saw Liz earlier. Confronted her about Jerry buying the bar."

"Wow. You haven't spoken with her for years. What did she say?"

"That she keeps her fingers out of his business deals. I believe her."

"That's good. Then you can put it away."

"Yeah."

He pulled into the parking lot of the same apartment building he'd lived in when he met Nikki.

Not much time had gone by—a couple of years—but he felt like he was running in place. He hadn't gotten far in those two years.

He hadn't changed.

Hadn't learned a damn thing.

"Dane? Are you still there?"

"Yeah. Just thinking. She said something interesting."

"You mean you had a conversation with her and not a screaming match?"

"That was part of it. When we were married, I never yelled, never raised my voice. She said she stomped all over me because I let her. After a while she lost respect for me, and that if I don't find a spine, Nikki will, too."

"I don't know enough about it to give you my opinion. You never wanted to talk about Liz."

"I said it was because it hurt, but remembering how she treated me was humiliating. That's why."

"So why bring all this up now? It's in the past, let it stay there. You have Nikki. Focus on that."

He rested his head against the backrest. "I don't remember us that way."

"We *weren't* that way. You did what you wanted. Always. You *never* sought my approval or asked for my permission to do anything. You didn't grovel to make me happy or do whatever I asked."

"What was different between me and Liz and between me and you?"

"Besides the fact I was happy with what little you gave me, and Liz wasn't?"

"Holly."

"What? It's true. I was a starving puppy under a table looking for scraps. If we're going to talk, we might as well be honest. Our roles were reversed. I did whatever I could to make you love me, and that included keeping my mouth shut about the way you treated me. You did whatever you could to make Liz happy. It's not hard to understand, Dane. People give up their power to the people they love. You didn't love me, but I loved you."

He swallowed past the lump in his throat. Holly hit the point he'd tried hard to find.

"Do you really think that's true?"

She let out a breath. "I don't know about your relationship with Liz, but if she said she wanted you to stand up for yourself, I'd believe it. Women want someone they can depend on. If you gave up your power in the relationship, maybe she felt like you were too weak to be an equal partner."

He sighed.

"It's not all on you, you know. Liz was demanding and unhappy. Had you stood up for yourself, well, you don't know if that would have helped. Maybe. Probably. It would have helped *you* at any rate. Your self-esteem wouldn't have taken such a beating."

That was definitely true. He'd come out of his divorce so broken he hadn't felt good enough for anyone. Something he still felt. He asked himself all the time what

Nikki saw in him that she would love him enough to marry him.

He'd belittled her, said some nasty things to her because he didn't have the guts to say what he really wanted to say.

"Thanks for talking to me," he said, unbuckling his seatbelt.

"You're welcome. I'm glad we're still friends. But Dane, if you listen to anything I say, listen to this. You have to let Liz go. You have to. Or she's going to destroy your marriage."

"I know. There's so much I've done, just in the past couple of weeks, that I'll never be able to take back. The bar is gone. My friendship with Brett may never be the same. Ian thinks he's not a good friend, competing with Brett for best friend of the year or some shit. How did my life get so fucked up?"

"Why are you so scared to tell anyone how you feel? Why do you keep hiding?"

"I guess I feel like my opinion doesn't matter, and I expect everyone to feel the same."

"Your opinion won't matter if you can't open your mouth. Liz has hurt you enough. Let her go."

"You're right. Goodnight, Holly."

"Goodnight, and good luck."

"Thanks."

Dane trotted up the stairs and let himself inside their small apartment. He wanted to give Nikki so much more than this. He bent and ran his hands over Princess Snowflake's fur. Her purring filled the kitchen.

He emptied his pockets and shuffled into the bedroom.

Nikki lay on her side, a pillow between her knees trying to find a comfortable position.

He stripped and slid into bed, spooning her from

behind. Her body radiated heat, and he molded his chest against her back.

He loved her so much.

If he didn't start showing her, she would leave.

Nikki wouldn't be like Holly. She loved him, but she wouldn't put up with him treating her poorly. It's why he loved her.

He smoothed his hand against her bump.

She gave everything she could to the people she loved. When she loved, she loved with her whole heart.

He had to start being who she needed him to be, or like Liz, she would find someone who would.

# NIKKI

Nikki's bladder woke her before the alarm did. She didn't need to set the darn thing, but she did anyway, just in case she managed to get a little sleep. The babies kicked around playing a lot of the night, finally settling down when Dane crawled into bed.

He'd surprised her when he cuddled on her. He did everything in his power to ignore the babies, pretend they didn't exist.

They hadn't spoken for a couple of days. The store was so busy, and when Dane started work on The Finish Line, the store had fallen squarely on her lap. She hired and kept stock. Ran the employee meetings and processed payroll.

She couldn't remember the last time Dane had come in, even to check things over. He trusted her completely. The only area of their lives where he did.

It could have been enough, but it wasn't.

Carefully as to not wake him or jostle the babies any more than necessary, she slid out of bed.

The race was only a few days away, and today she and Margie would be taking care of the bulk of the customers.

She needed the extra help. She took more breaks than she used to, to eat and make sure she kept herself hydrated and to get off her feet.

Dane didn't see the extra payroll expenses, and they wouldn't last long.

After using the bathroom, she started a pot of decaf coffee. She'd made the change easily enough, though Stacy constantly reminded her there were better things she could drink. Luckily for her, Jack kept Stacy from harping on her too much.

Dane would be glad when these babies were born, but for Nikki, that day couldn't come soon enough.

In a hurry to fall into bed, he'd left his wallet and phone on the counter. She picked it up, intending to set it on the nightstand where he could reach for it later. The phone woke up, and his notifications flashed across the screen.

Holly's name blinked at the top, and she tilted the phone to keep it from disappearing.

*Thanks for the call last night. XO*

Dane still spoke to Holly.

Slim and beautiful, Holly was a gorgeous redhead with brilliant green eyes. She'd never met Holly in person, but Marta had become friends with her before she'd moved to New Hampshire for a teaching opportunity.

Obviously, Dane missed her and the no-strings relationship he'd had with her. He'd probably told her how fat and ugly she'd become carrying her sister's babies.

Tears dripped down her cheeks.

She dried her eyes and placed the phone on the nightstand.

With her stomach churning, she skipped the coffee and dressed for her shift.

Not her store.

Not her babies.

Not her husband, either, if he was still spending time talking to his ex-girlfriend behind her back.

She forced herself to eat something for the babies and drove to work. Somehow she opened the store, put on a happy face for the customers. Chatted about the marathon and what a great job Marta was doing, talked about the babies, endured people putting their hands on her, patting her bump and guessing their genders.

Normally she didn't care, almost enjoyed the attention the babies brought her, but today she wanted to be left alone.

Alyssa came in an hour before she planned to go. Margie had been urging her to leave all day, but she stuck it out.

"Hi," Alyssa said as Nikki restocked protein bars.

"Hey."

Alyssa bit her bottom lip. "Are you mad at me?"

She glanced at her friend out of the corner of her eyes, but concentrated on the bars, centering them just so. If she lost control for one second, she'd fall apart.

"No. Tired. What's up? Where's Drew?"

"I left him with Sadie for a while. He's playing with Hannah and Shyla."

She forced herself to smile. "That's nice."

"I haven't seen you for a while. How are you?"

"Fine. Same as always."

Alyssa blew out a sigh and adjusted the strap of her large bag. "You *are* mad at me. I'm sorry Brett caused so many problems wanting to get out of The Finish Line."

Her eyes filled with tears. "It's not that."

"Sweetie. Then what is it?"

"Let's not talk here."

Nikki gathered the empty boxes and plastic wrap to throw away. "I'm taking a fifteen," she told Margie.

"You should go home," she said as she rang up a customer buying a new pair of running shoes.

"I have a few more things to do first. I'll be in the office if you need me."

Alyssa followed her into the small space. "I agree with Margie. You look beat."

"Pretty soon. Dane can spend more time here again, and the marathon will be over in a few days. It's always been a busy time of year." She lowered herself into Dane's office chair and rubbed her hands over her belly in soothing circles. Her lower back ached. "I think Dane's cheating on me with Holly."

Her friend's cheeks pinked, and Nikki froze.

"Why do you think that?" Alyssa asked.

"I moved his phone to the bedroom this morning. Holly texted him. Thanking him for a phone call." She paused and studied Alyssa's face. She knew guilt when she saw it. "You knew."

Running her fingers through her hair in agitation, Alyssa said, "Brett caught him talking to someone a few nights ago. He didn't know it was Holly."

Her body went from hot to cold and back to burning up in the space of a few seconds. Her hands started shaking. "You knew. You knew and didn't tell me."

"We didn't know it was Holly."

"Does that make a difference? You knew he was talking to another woman."

"Holly lives in New Hampshire. What harm can she do from there? Unless, is she back in town?"

"I don't know. I never see Dane anymore. Our schedules are too different, and the bigger I get, the more he avoids me." She hefted to her feet. "I need to go."

"Let me help—"

She jerked away from Alyssa's outstretched hand. "You've done enough."

"Nikki."

She grabbed her purse. "Don't 'Nikki' me. Brett heard Dane talking to another woman, and everyone knows about it except me. How am I supposed to feel?"

Leaning against the doorjamb, she took several deep breaths. She had to calm down.

"Let me drive you home. You're upset."

"Why do you think that is? Don't do me any favors."

She stopped at the counter. "I'm taking your advice and going home. Call Dane if you need something. I need to rest."

Margie frowned. "Are you okay?"

"No, I'm not. But don't worry about it."

She hurried out of the Tower City Running Company.

Stupid store. It's what started this whole mess. Where would she be if she'd accepted that job offer at Shine? Dated Eric? Let him—

She wiped her eyes.

Dumb.

Alyssa stood outside the store watching her.

It pissed her off Alyssa knew Dane had been talking to Holly and never said anything. Brett knew, and he probably told Ian which meant Marta knew.

She was the laughingstock of the group.

Dane calling his ex.

God.

Tears ran in streams from her eyes and she could barely see to throw her purse into the passenger's seat and settle behind the wheel.

She cranked the air conditioner.

She'd never been so angry at Alyssa than she was right now. Gripping the wheel, she pushed down the childish urge to give her best friend the finger as she drove by.

Focusing on the road, she drove carefully the whole way home. She didn't want to endanger herself or Stacy's babies.

Dane's truck wasn't in the parking lot when she pulled up, and she said a quick prayer in thanks. If he wanted Holly, he could have her. The next time they talked could be through her divorce attorney. At least they didn't have children to fight over.

Nikki took a few minutes to feed Princess Snowflake and give her fresh water. She gulped a glass of cold water, too, and pressed an ice-cold washcloth to her forehead.

Overheating. High blood pressure. She needed to relax or she'd be hospitalized with pre-eclampsia.

Her parents would take care of her and after she spent a few days resting, she could spend the remaining months with Stacy. Give Dane room to reacquaint himself with Holly. He wouldn't have to hide to talk to her anymore.

In the bedroom, she found her suitcase and her hands shook as she started dumping clothes into it. She didn't care what she packed.

Maternity blouses, shorts, leggings. Huge granny panties. No wonder Dane couldn't stand to look at her. No matter how much lotion she rubbed into her belly, stretch marks would always mar her skin. Remind her of what she'd given up so Stacy could be a mother. Her body would never be the same.

She choked back a sob.

"What are you doing?"

She jumped when Dane stepped into the room, panic filling his eyes when he saw the open suitcase on their bed.

"I'm leaving. What does it look like I'm doing?" She kept her voice steady even though she wanted to melt into a blubbering puddle on the floor at his feet.

He looked so good dressed in slacks and a dress shirt. Scruff covered his jaw, and his hair was mussed. It was her favorite look on him, and it took all her willpower not to cave in.

"Why?"

She had to give him points for looking like he cared.

"I know you've been talking to Holly. Hell, our whole group knows, and I had to find out by accident? Because I was being thoughtful and moved your phone to the bedroom. I know what I look like, and I know how you feel about me. Let's just cut the crap for once, okay? I'll get out of your face and take Stacy's babies with me. You do what you want to do. Date Holly again since she gave you what you needed after all."

She slammed her suitcase closed.

"Nik, please don't do this. You don't know what you saw."

Pulling the suitcase from the bed, she scoffed. "I know what Xs and Os mean. I'm not stupid."

"She signs all her texts like that."

"Good for her."

He stood in front of the door, and she stopped in front of him, her suitcase at her feet. "Let me by."

"No."

"You don't want me here. You haven't spoken two words to me in weeks. We're as far apart as two people can possibly be, and we've been married less than a year. A divorce should be simple. Keep your share of The Finish Line. Take the store. I don't want anything that belongs to you."

"None of that matters. I love you. Won't you at least let me explain?"

"Explain what? Let me go."

"I can't. Don't you understand it would kill me if you left me?"

"Maybe you should have thought of that before talking to your ex-girlfriend. I'm sure she's still just as gorgeous as ever, and I'm this huge hippo who can barely move. When I get settled at my parents', I'll come back for my cat. I can't take her right now, and I'm sorry if she bothers you."

Somehow thinking about leaving Princess Snowflake behind made her cry, and she tipped her head back, hoping it would help keep the tears at bay.

He reached out to touch her, and she shrank back. "Let me go."

Something in him shifted, and his eyes hardened, his mouth thinned. He'd never gotten mad at her, and she took a step back. "No. I'm not letting you leave until you hear what I have to say."

The day spent at the store and the stuffy air of the apartment pushed at her, and light-headed, she swayed on her feet.

So tired. She was so tired.

"Nikki. God, you went all white. Come into the living room."

She let him lead her into the other room, and he turned on their air conditioning unit. Gratefully, she sank onto the sofa and closed her eyes.

When she opened them, he'd set a cold glass of water on

the coffee table, and he sat next to her, taking her clammy hand in his. "Do you need to go to the doctor? When is your next appointment?"

She jerked her hand away. "I had an appointment earlier this week. My mom went with me because you were at the bar. You never cared and I stopped pretending you did."

His arm shot out, and he gripped her chin in his hand. "You want to know why? Because I'm trying not to get too attached to these babies. I see you day after day, your body growing with babies that *aren't mine*. The family you're creating *isn't mine*. And I'm dealing with that the only way I know how."

Misery covered his face, his eyes shimmering with moisture.

"Why didn't you say something?"

He dropped his hand, but she could still feel his fingertips digging into her skin.

"What am I supposed to say that doesn't turn me into a selfish prick?" With a gentler touch, he brushed the stray hair from her ponytail away from her cheek. "I admire you so much for doing what you're doing. For the time, the discomfort, the health risks. To give your sister and her husband what they've tried so hard for years to make for themselves. I can't imagine how hard Jack has had it, trying to be strong for Stacy. He wanted a family just as much as Stacy does but he couldn't say one thing because he wanted all his energy to be there for his wife. There was no way I was going to stop that."

"I would have preferred not doing this at all had I known what it would do to us," she said. "My marriage is important to me. *You* are important to me."

"I didn't know how I would feel, and even if I had, I'm

not in the habit of speaking up, of communicating my needs to other people. Liz taught me that what I wanted, what I needed, didn't matter, and I'm still learning that it's okay to say something. To disagree. That it won't be the end of the world if you want to do something and I don't want you to do it or vice versa. Compromise is a foreign concept to me because I've never been in a relationship where I had it."

"This is a nice talk, but it's six months too late." She struggled to her feet. "I think we need a break. I'm going to live with Stacy until the babies are born. When I come back, you can tell me if you want to give this another shot, or if I should find my own place."

"I'm not letting you go."

"You can't tell me what to do." She lifted her chin.

He sagged into the sofa and her heart hitched.

"What if I asked you not to go?"

"Tell me why you were talking to Holly. Do you want her back?"

Dane sprang to his feet. "No! The only reason I called her—" With his hands on his hips, he paced in a small circle. "I saw Liz, too. I confronted her about Overland's offer. She said she didn't have anything to do with that."

"That doesn't have anything to do with us, or Stacy's babies. If you're going to take me on a ride—"

"I'm trying to explain and doing a crappy job. I don't want you to go. Will you wait until I get it all out?"

Nikki sucked in a breath. The air conditioning was working, and the cool air washed over her. He was trying to explain. It's more than he'd done in a while, and she owed it to him to listen.

Running never solved anything, and she couldn't let it be her go-to defense mechanism whenever he made her unhappy. She had to remember she loved this man, knew the baggage he carried and loved him anyway.

"Okay. I promise to hear you out." She sat on the couch, pulled a throw blanket into her lap, and scratched at Princess Snowflake's fur as she listened.

DANE

Thank God. He hadn't lost her . . . yet. He died a million times watching her pack. Driving her away because he was a cowardly asshole. If he would have opened his mouth from the beginning, none of this would have happened.

He stayed on his feet, too nervous and anxious to sit.

"I went to see Liz and I asked her why she married me."

"I'm guessing because she loved you," Nikki said, her fingers twisted in her lap.

"She said she did, but we went to shit so fast."

"I feel her there," she mumbled.

"She said she lost respect for me because I turned into a doormat. All I wanted was to make her happy. I don't know how that could have been wrong, but it was."

"Because when you do what someone tells you to do and you don't want to do it, you lose respect for yourself. You hated yourself for giving in just as much as she hated you. I saw that when we met."

"You're right. And I called Holly. I asked her why we didn't have that kind of relationship. I could see it starting with you. Barely a year in, and already our marriage is turning into what I had with Liz. Do you know what she said?"

"No."

"She said it was because I didn't love her. And that's when it clicked for me. I give control to the people I care about so they don't stop loving me."

"Dane."

He sniffled, huffed a laugh. "Good thing Holly's a soci-ology expert. I may never have figured it out on my own, but she's right. I gave Liz whatever she wanted because I loved her. When you said you wanted to surrogate for Stacy, I agreed. I didn't want to disappoint you, Nik. I love you so much and we'd only been married six months. I wanted to make you happy, and it did. But as the babies grew, I became so miserable."

Nikki struggled to her feet, and he helped her, taking her hand. She rested her head on his shoulder and he wrapped his arms around her, the babies between them the way they've been since the infertility specialist implanted them into her uterus.

"Tell me how you really feel about these babies. No lies, no qualifiers. I want to know the truth."

"The truth is, I'm proud of you. I'm proud that you would do this for your family. I don't have brothers or sisters so I don't understand that bond, but I am a man and watching Jack struggle because he wanted to be a father—I can relate to that. I want kids, someday. I really do," he said when she looked at him with her huge blue eyes shining with tears.

"I want these babies to be ours. I was disappointed when you said you wanted to do this, that the first baby you would carry wouldn't belong to us. But I love you for your courage and your strength. Stacy is lucky to have you for a sister, and I'm very fortunate you're my wife."

A sense of déjà vu washed over him, and he shivered. Eighteen months ago he'd vowed in this very room to never give her another reason to run away from him. Yet he had, and he'd almost lost her again.

"I'm sorry, too. When I thought of it, I got so excited. I didn't give us much of a chance to talk about it. We should have taken time to have those discussions, and I'm sorry for my part in this."

"You didn't have to say that, but I appreciate it. The way I handle things affects not just you. We lost the bar because Ian thought I didn't want to run it without Brett. I let Ian do what he wanted, and he sold it. I don't tell people anything because I'm used to being ignored. Liz never listened, my parents never listened when I tried to explain what happened between me and Liz. I learned to keep my mouth shut."

"And I didn't listen because having Stacy's babies was something I wanted to do." She rested her hands on his.

His hands had found their way to her belly, the twins moving under his palms. One day they would share this, and the baby moving would belong to them.

"You're worried about having to give them up?" she asked.

"A little. Yeah. I've been trying to not get attached and I'm worried for you."

"I get it. Maybe it's different somehow, but they don't feel like mine. Maybe I've been able to distance myself. I'm not sure."

"I've been talking to my therapist—"

"You've been doing a lot of talking," she said, a small smile turning up the corners of her mouth.

He traced one of her lips with is fingertip.

"I have been. There are surrogate support groups. Would you like to join one? Talk to other couples, compare notes? It might help me to have other people to relate to."

"That would be great." She paused. "I'm proud of you, too. For putting in the work. For going back and trying to figure out what went wrong. It paid off, and now we can adjust, move forward."

"Holly did say one more thing."

Nikki stilled in his arms.

"It's not bad, but probably the most truthful thing anyone has said. I need to let Liz go. She didn't ask her husband to buy the bar, and even if she had, it shouldn't have mattered. I need to forget about her, or I'm going to lose you. She's taken enough away from me."

"I agree, but she was your first wife, and you loved her. It's okay to feel a sense of loss, or maybe failure. It's important to learn from it and move on. What are we going to do now?"

"I've been thinking about that, too."

"Really? Do you know what you want to do now that The Finish Line is gone?"

"You said Stacy wants you to live with her so she can experience the last month of your pregnancy with you, right?"

"Yeah, but I knew I couldn't do that."

"What if we moved?"

She blinked. "To Chicago?"

When he'd first thought of it, he'd felt a spark. A fizz in his blood. New beginnings. Leave the past behind.

"Exactly. I think it's fate I didn't say anything to Ian. I'm glad he sold the bar, but I would have been equally happy if he wouldn't have and I left it up to him. I didn't think he'd draw the conclusions he did about our friendship, but that's a different conversation that I'll need to have with him one day. Anyway, now that we're free—"

Nikki laughed. "I think you forgot about the store."

Dane grinned. "Oh, ye of little faith. I have it all worked out. But let's get off our feet. You need to rest."

He urged her down the hall and they crawled onto the bed, lay face to face.

"You really want to move to Chicago?" she asked after he laid out his entire plan.

"My mom and dad might be a little disappointed, but we have to do what's best for us. I like Stacy and Jack and I know you would love to live near them."

"Is this about the babies?" she asked as he caressed her skin under her maternity blouse.

"Partly. I know I'm only their uncle, but I would like to watch them grow up. Live nearby when Stacy and Jack need a sitter. I love them, your body is growing them, and they share your DNA. That makes them mine, too. A part of our family."

"Stacy will faint. She's wanted me to move for years."

"It'll be good for us, Nik."

"Won't you miss Brett and Ian?"

"They've moved on to wives and kids, and they'll be looking at different career opportunities. I don't want to say there's no room in their lives for us, but friendships are secondary to family."

"Alyssa and I haven't felt very close, either. I blamed her for not telling me about you talking to Holly."

"Don't be mad at her for that, but you're right. Her loyalty lies with Brett, and it should, shouldn't it?"

"Yeah, I guess so."

"We have time to talk more about it. We both learned

not to jump into anything, and we'll take a look at our budget, where we would live, that kind of thing, before we say anything to anyone."

She scrubbed her fingers through his whiskers. "I like it."

"Good. Now, I think a nap is in order, some pizza, and a little Flix Roulette. What do you think?"

"I think I love you."

He rested his forehead against hers. She forgave so easily. "I'm sorry I was stupid."

"I'm sorry I didn't take the time to listen."

He scooted closer, tangling his legs with hers, pushing his arm under her pillow. She looked so beautiful with her hair in fluffy curls around her head, and love without doubt shining in her eyes.

"Is this okay?" he whispered, leaning in, his lips feathering against hers.

"Definitely."

He nudged her mouth open and slipped his tongue inside. He loved the taste of her, the way she wrapped her arms around his neck.

She had such a big heart, and she loved him.

He pulled away and pressed a kiss to the babies.

His niece and nephew.

Adjusting a blanket around them, he tucked her into his side. "Get some sleep. You need it."

"Don't go anywhere," she said, her eyelids already drooping in exhaustion.

"I won't. You have me forever. I promise."

"Dane wants to go for a run," Brett said, looking up from his phone.

He grimaced. Sitting on the floor with Drew, they'd been building with blocks while Alyssa puttered around in the kitchen. It was the kind of evening he'd dreamed about when he and Alyssa planned their family.

"You don't want to talk to him?"

"It's the running part that sucks."

Alyssa laughed. "Maybe a taste of your own medicine would be good for you."

"Gee, thanks."

"You should go. Nikki's still pissed at me, and I'll need to talk to her, too. There's nothing worse than having a friend mad at you."

"Dane's been off the rails. I hope he's not going to tell me he and Nikki are getting a divorce."

She twisted her mouth. "I'd like to think I know Nikki better than that. She's not one to give up so easily."

"If anyone needs someone with grit, it's Dane. He doesn't know his head from his ass most days."

"Go talk to him. Drew and I will hang out. What can it hurt?"

"Like I said, the talking isn't what I'm worried about."

"Pussy."

"Funny, that's what he said."

Alyssa sat next to him on the floor and took a block Drew held out to her.

He nuzzled her temple with his nose. "Thank you."

"Save that for later. You might want to take it back when you can't walk tomorrow."

*Ain't that the truth*, Brett thought as he laced up his shoes and bounded outside.

Dane walked toward him on the path, his long strides eating up the pavement.

Jesus Christ.

Dane was going to kick his ass.

"Take it easy on me," he said when Dane stepped into earshot.

"When have I ever?" He grinned.

"Fuck."

Dane laughed, slapping him on the stomach. "Come on."

They started out, letting other runners pass who were getting in a last long run before the race. Once Brett had stopped directing the marathon, he'd stopped running it, too. It had never occurred to him to register to race, more content to spend time with Drew and Alyssa than log his miles on the trails.

Mile after mile went by, and he wondered if Dane had intended to talk to him at all, or if this had been a ploy to kill him and leave his body in the middle of the park to be ravaged by deadly squirrels.

As another mile went by, he was sure Dane had plotted his demise by heart attack.

"How long we going?" he asked, panting after mile five.

Dane slowed to a walk. "Sorry. I got caught up."

"You sound good."

"I feel good. Nik and I, we're solid. We had a good talk a couple days ago. Would have saved us some hurt if we would have done it sooner, but I wasn't in a place where I could have. I think on some level she understands that too. I'm lucky she puts up with me."

"Good. I never got behind you talking to Holly."

"I know, and Nikki didn't either. I needed it, and I explained what Holly made me realize about my part in my divorce and my dead-end relationship with her. Nikki understood, and now that part's done. I want to talk to you about something."

He walked alongside his best friend since high school. They'd gone through so much shit together, but he felt their lives shifting. Things change, seasons drew to a close and new opportunities came their way. People grew apart, new relationships formed.

Dane was moving on. He could tell in his friend's tone, by the way he carried himself.

And as much as Brett hated it, he expected it. He could only hope it didn't hurt too much.

"Okay."

A family of four rode their bikes past them, and Dane waited to speak until they were out of range.

"Nikki and I are moving to Chicago."

The spit in his mouth dried up leaving him fumbling for words. "What?"

"To be closer to Stacy and Jack, before the babies are born.

We don't want to see our niece and nephew once or twice a year. Nikki wants time with her sister, and Jack's become a good friend of mine. Liz chewed me up and spit me out, and a change of scenery will help me forget the whole thing."

"But . . ." He struggled for something to say that didn't make him sound like a pansy picked last in gym class. "But what about Ian and Marta?"

*What about me?* he wanted to ask.

"We'll still be friends. Chicago's only six hours away. We'll take road trips and spend weekends here. My parents will still be here. We've talked about it. A lot. Made sure it's what we both want."

"Then I'm happy for you. What will you do for work?"

"I'm not sure yet. This past year took a lot out of me, you know? I need to regroup, help Nikki recover after the babies are born. She'll probably have a cesarean section, and she might need a few weeks to heal."

"Alyssa needed months."

"I remember, and I want to be there for Nikki if she needs the same. I can find a nine-to-five somewhere. I'm not as worried about it as I used to be."

Brett agreed. There was a calm about Dane that hadn't been there before. A peace. He'd gotten something out of talking to Holly and Liz and if he and Nikki were stronger than ever, all he could do was be happy for them.

"What about your store?"

"That's why I wanted to talk to you. I don't want to sell it if I don't have to, but it's going to need a manager. I want to offer you the job. I can pay you what I pay Nikki, maybe a little more. I have a solid staff, thanks to the time Nikki's put in, but I can't say you won't have to work some evenings and weekends every once in a while. It won't be as grueling as The Finish Line, though."

"What will you do if I say no?"

Dane shrugged. "Not sure. I could offer the position to Margie again, maybe she would take it now. Or if it came to that, I'd see if Overland wanted it. Even if he didn't keep it as a running shoe store, the area is prime, and he might want the building for something else. Like I said, I'm not worried about it. For the first time in a long time, I don't care about trivial stuff. Nikki almost left me. If I would have come back to the apartment fifteen minutes later, ten, she would have been gone, and I don't know what would have happened. She listened to me, she believed me, and she loves me. Seriously, when you look at Alyssa, you know that's the only thing that matters."

"Yeah."

It sounded so unlike Dane, but his face was free of wrinkles, his eyes unclouded. He'd found his place after all this time, after fighting all his demons.

"I'd need to talk to Alyssa about it."

Dane kicked at a rock on the sidewalk. "I'm sorry I was a dick. I said those things out of jealousy. I've always admired you, respected you. What you made of yourself."

"Alyssa helped a lot with that. I'd probably still be living in that crummy studio if it weren't for her. She made me realize I was worth something. Even if my parents didn't."

"Yeah, but you gave her the chance in the first place."

Brett started to run. "I didn't want to. When she ran off to Florida I tried to live without her. That didn't work very well." He shivered. Remembering the way he'd suffered after he'd lost her churned his stomach and desperately he batted the feeling away. "Come on. I'll race you back."

"Can you handle that?"

"Things are good. I can handle whatever comes my way."

Dane hooted, and it echoed across the park. "We'll see about that."

Brett chased Dane down the sidewalk, his heart hammering. Alyssa waited for him, and his little boy. Dane was right. When it came to anything that mattered, his family was what mattered most.

He picked up speed and shot Dane the bird as he flew past.

Dane gave chase, and Brett howled in laughter.

He'd always have his friendship with Dane.

And that mattered, too.

# IAN

Ian rolled over, blinking the sun out of his eyes. He wasn't alone, and he pulled Marta to him, her body heavy in sleep.

With the race over, she'd allowed herself the luxury of sleeping in. Sleeping in meant barely eight these days, especially with a little devil-child who demanded breakfast before the sun rose for the day, but Shyla's bed was empty. Sadie was awake and the little girl was probably sitting downstairs watching morning cartoons while she dug into a bowl of cereal or eggs if Sadie decided to cook.

Ian nibbled along Marta's jaw. He should let her sleep, but he seldom had her in bed alone without interruptions. He wouldn't be a man if he didn't take advantage of it.

She opened her eyes and smiled sleepily.

God, she turned him on.

"Hey, good morning."

"Hey, good morning to you, too." His lips continued their exploration down her neck and over the tops of her breasts.

"Do we have time for this?" she asked, running her fingers through his hair.

"No," he mumbled, making her laugh. "But that won't stop me."

"It will if Shyla comes in wanting to know if she's going to daycare today."

"Is she?"

"No. I'm keeping her and Hannah while Sadie runs to campus, and Nikki and Alyssa are coming over. Alyssa's bringing Drew for a playdate. Let's have everyone over for dinner tonight."

"Good plan. The guys can help me put Shyla's play equipment together."

"We can talk while you all play with your power tools. I think they have things to say."

He propped himself onto an elbow. "Who? Alyssa and Nikki? To you?"

"Not me, specifically. And I want to know how things turned out between Nikki and Dane. Holly called me and she said she's been talking to Dane a lot lately, helping him sort things out."

"You knew about that? And you didn't say anything?"

"What was there to say? They parted as friends. Why can't they talk to each other?"

"You don't think Dane is cheating on Nikki with her?"

Marta moved away from him, and he missed her heat. "Of course not. She never said anything about that."

He scoffed. "She wouldn't have told you."

"No, I guess not, but I know Dane, and before she moved away, I got to know Holly a little too. They're only friends."

"Like you're friends with Brett." He couldn't help it.

She could have gotten mad. She could have rolled out of

bed and slammed into the bathroom. Instead, she inched toward him, wrapped her arms around his neck.

He sighed. "I'm sorry. I can't seem to stop myself from poking at you."

"I know, and I understand. Let's get married this summer."

He lowered his head and pressed his lips softly to hers. "I would really like that."

"Good." She grabbed his cock through his boxers. "Now shut up and poke me with something else."

"We don't have time."

"We have five minutes. Show me whatcha got, hot stuff."

And he did.

Ian stood outside The Finish Line. His stomach twisted, and perspiration beaded on his skin. Though the temperature hadn't made it to seventy degrees Fahrenheit, sweat dripped down his back.

It was done.

It hadn't seemed real until he signed the papers, shook hands, accepted the congratulations.

Dane had stood stiff, unwilling to shake Overland's hand, but he'd done it, made the deal.

The Finish Line no longer belonged to them.

The transition had been smooth, and the waitstaff and Bobbi had been sorry to see them go. They'd been fun to work with, she said, and she would miss them. It had taken him a minute to thank her, give her a hug without crying.

He hadn't figured it would hurt this much.

It wasn't the bar he'd miss, though, it would be the

friendships, the camaraderie. The connection he'd had with Brett and Dane during the good times.

Brett drove across the parking lot in his beat-up car, and Ian slid his sunglasses over his face. Brett didn't need to see his bloodshot eyes.

As he leaned against his car, the manager Overland hired unlocked the door for the early lunch crowd.

This would be the last time he'd be here. He wouldn't be able to sit and eat a meal without feeling a sense of loss of what his future could have been like had they held onto it.

Brett climbed out of his car and slammed the door. "You okay?"

Ian shrugged. "Yeah. I guess so. I'm going to miss this place."

"I hear you. But Christ, did she take up a lot of time."

"Yeah."

Ian hooked his thumbs into his belt loops. There wasn't a whole lot more to say that hadn't already been said, and he wondered why Brett followed him down the strip from Overland's office.

"You hear Dane and Nikki are moving to Chicago?" Brett asked.

Ian anchored a foot to his bumper. "Nope. They're moving closer to Stacy and Jack?"

"Yeah. And I think Dane wants to put some space between him and his exes."

"Don't blame him."

"No, but the thing is, he offered me the manager job at his store."

"Nice fit for you."

And it just cemented his thoughts that Dane and Brett would always be better friends. He wasn't hurt Dane hadn't mentioned anything to him. Hell, the last thing he wanted was to manage a running shoe store. But no one told him Dane and Nikki were moving, either, and that bit him in the ass more than he wanted it to.

"That's the thing. I told Dane I would think about it, but Alyssa and I talked and we're going to stay in Florida for a bit. Not for good, not like Dane and Nikki and Chicago, but for a while. Alyssa's mom and stepdad want some time with Drew, and after this past year, I would like some stress-free time with her. You know. I'm sure you're looking forward to a lazy summer with Marta."

"Sure."

"I haven't talked to Dane about it, but I was wondering if you wanted to manage it? I think he'd prefer someone he trusted in that position, especially since one of his old employees tried to rob it a couple years ago."

Ian was shaking his head before Brett finished talking. "No. That's not my thing, but thanks."

"Shit. I don't want to tell him I don't want to do it. What about Marta?"

"Marta . . . well, you'd have to ask her. She wants to talk to you, anyway. She's done with the marathon. She can't run anymore and she wants to put it behind her."

"I figured she would. It's okay. Before Alyssa and I take off, I'll help her find a replacement. I know the players better than she does. She doesn't have to feel bad."

"She was worried about disappointing you."

"It's cool. Looks like we're all going our separate ways."

"Looks like it."

Brett paused for a moment. "You still hate me, don't you?"

Ian took his sunglasses off and looked Brett in the eye. "I never hated you. That wouldn't be fair. What you and

Marta had back then was none of my business. But we're talking straight?"

"Yeah."

"Then I'll tell you straight. I'll always resent you for having her first. I know it's irrational, I know it doesn't make sense. I have exes she doesn't give a shit about, but you have always been under my skin. We had a good time working this old girl," he said, tilting his head toward the bar, "but that part of our lives is over now. No one to blame, and maybe it's for the best. All I want to do is move on with Marta. We're getting married this summer, and if you were smart, you'd keep your mouth shut about it."

Brett chuckled, smirked, and then let out a long sigh. "I want nothing but the best for her, and she has that with you. The last thing I'm going to do is interfere, and there's no reason for me to. Alyssa and I are getting married, too. On the beach. Don't plan yours the same weekend we have ours. I'd like you to be there."

"Who the fuck said I wanted to go?" Ian asked, but he laughed.

"I did, you asshole. Come on, I'll buy you a drink."

"Now?"

"Yeah."

"You don't want to invite Dane?"

"Nah. You and me. Let's bury the hatchet once and for all."

"You know what? That sounds good." He held out his hand, and Brett shook it, long and firm.

Ian followed Brett into the bar.

It was a closure of sorts, in a few different ways. He could put Brett's relationship with Marta behind him, no turning back. He could stop poking at her, and start poking at her the other way, which was a lot more fun, and she'd enjoyed it a lot more, too.

Maybe he'd feel guilty for being the slightest bit glad Brett and Alyssa were going to spend some time in Florida, but he'd think about it later.

For now, he'd have a cold one with Brett and count his blessings.

Having good friends was one of them.

# MARTA

Marta answered the door with Hannah attached to her hip, the baby's sticky fingers twisted in her hair. After Hannah's birth, Marta had worried she and Sadie would stop getting along. She tried to keep out of Sadie's way, let her be Hannah's mother, but Sadie asked for help, and now the two women co-mothered Hannah in a way that worked for both of them. She thought of the baby as her granddaughter, and she nurtured Sadie as she would her own daughter.

It took a village, and Marta was more than happy to be a part of it.

Shyla danced around her legs, eager to play with Drew.

"Back up so they can come in," she said, opening the door to Alyssa and Nikki who had driven together.

Hunter came in behind them, and Shyla buried her face in the dog's fur.

"The guys are still out back. They're almost done with the play equipment."

"Thanks for having us over," Nikki said, holding out a cheesecake from the grocery store.

"We thought it would be fun to have one last party," Marta said closing the door behind them.

Alyssa set Drew to his feet, and Shyla hugged him, giving him a smack on the cheek.

"She's going to miss him," Marta said.

"It won't be forever. I contacted a realtor, and she's going to list my condo for rent. My mother helped us secure an apartment not far from her house and we signed a year lease. She's so excited." Alyssa hung her purse on the coat tree near the door.

"Come into the living room. I made lemonade and there's coffee. Decaf, too, if you're in the mood, Nik. I bought some sparkling grape juice, and if you're hungry, I have a meat and cheese tray I can put out."

"You've thought of everything," Nikki said, lowering herself into a recliner.

"I'm going to put Hunter outside with the guys." Alyssa nudged the dog into the backyard where they were putting together a huge play structure made up of a fort, swings, and a spiral slide. "That thing is enormous."

"Ian bought it for the girls with part of the money from the sale. They're going to have a lot of fun once it's all put together. We appreciate the guys helping. Ian would never have been able to do it himself."

"It's good practice," Nikki said watching Dane help Ian secure the plastic slide to the side of the fort.

"Nothing like putting together a bike on Christmas Eve." That's exactly what Ian had done for Shyla last year and she'd been over the moon when she'd found the trike on Christmas morning, a big red bow attached to the handlebars.

The kids were on the floor playing with giant puzzles and Marta served her friends coffee and put out a tray of crackers and cheese. She sat on the arm of the sofa with a mug of coffee and said, "I'm sorry I didn't tell you Dane was talking to Holly. Ian kind of read me the riot act, but honestly, I didn't see anything bad in it. I've known Dane for many, many years, and the last thing I thought when Holly told me about their conversations was that he was cheating on you."

"It's fine. I was mad at Alyssa, *really* mad, but we worked it out. Dane explained, and I see his point. He's been working so hard to learn from his mistakes, and that's why I think moving to Chicago will be good for us. My parents are thinking of moving, too. My mom wants to be close to help Stacy with the twins, and she doesn't want to miss a second of being a grandma. She's looked forward to this for a long time."

She stared into her coffee cup. She wasn't as close to Nikki and Alyssa as Ian was to Brett and Dane. They had a history that she didn't share with the women sitting in her living room, and though she would miss them, for her the summer would be more about moving past running, what the sport had given her, and taken away. "It feels like things aren't going to be the same. When he got here, Dane asked me if I wanted to manage his store, and I said no. I'm not sure what he's going to do with it, but I'm not interested in being a part of the running community anymore."

"He's going to sell it. He has an appointment later this week to talk to Jerry about a deal. He knew Brett wouldn't end up taking the position, and instead of sulking, he did something about it. I'm proud of him. In the past I think he would have stewed over it to the point of blowing up. He's come a long way."

Marta winced. "I'm sorry for my part in that."

Nikki smiled. "Don't be. I would never say so but

keeping the store here while trying to live in Chicago would be like straddling a fence, and I'm relieved it worked out this way. Now we have a clean slate, and after these babies are born, and I heal up, we'll start our own family."

"What are you and Ian going to do, then? No marathon, no store, no bar," Alyssa asked.

"With the sale and my settlement, we have a little bit of cash and we don't have to decide right away. We want to get married this summer, and we'll take a vacation when you and Brett tie the knot. We need the break, and I haven't said anything to Ian yet but I'm checking into having my tubal ligation reversed. It might not work, but it's been in the back of my mind to at least go in and have a consultation."

Nikki lumbered to her feet and gave her a hug. "That's fantastic news. I'm happy for you, and I wish you all the luck in the world."

"Thanks. Fingers crossed. Let's sit outside. It looks like the guys are done, and Shyla can give the equipment her seal of approval."

Nikki herded the kids outside, giving Hannah a boost, the baby molding herself around her bump. Taking his hand, Shyla helped Drew through the door and Brett swung him onto the grass.

Hunter sniffed around the yard for the perfect place to pee.

Ian lifted the grill cover and turned on the propane.

Marta lifted her hand in acknowledgement and went into the kitchen to prepare the meat for the grill. She had chicken soaking in barbecue sauce, seasoned steaks, and Shyla's favorite turkey dogs.

"Hey," Alyssa said, following her into the kitchen.

Marta raised her eyebrows. "Hey?"

Alyssa laughed. "I know how that sounded. I wanted to

say, you know, I'm sorry for the way I treated you when we met. I wanted Brett so badly. I was afraid he was still in love with you and that you were going to ruin everything."

"You aren't the only one who felt that way. Ian had a tough time believing there isn't anything between Brett and me anymore. Nothing except a painful history and a shaky friendship. The way he plays with Drew . . . I see that and get choked up. He wouldn't have been a father like that to our baby. The more time he spends with Drew, the more I know I did the right thing. And sometimes doing the right thing hurts."

"Like going our separate ways."

"When Ian told me you and Brett were moving to Florida for a while, he tried to hide it, but there was relief. Splitting up the group will hurt, but for us as couples, I think we need the space."

"I'm glad you don't resent that."

"What is there to resent? Ian wanting me for himself? You and Brett finally getting married, or him being the kind of father to your child that he wouldn't have been with mine? Dane and Nikki making a life in a different city? Time goes on and things change. It might take a little more work, but the guys have been buddies since high school. They won't let a little distance keep them from being friends."

"And you really are okay with me and Brett?"

Marta gave Alyssa a hug. "I think you saved him. I think you saved him in a way no one could have. I can see it when I look at you two together. You're perfect for him. Don't doubt it anymore."

"You guys talking about me?" Brett asked, walking across the living room.

"Of course we are. Since you're here, can you take this

out to Ian?" she asked, holding up the platter of meat for the grill.

"Yep. Nikki asked for a bottle of water."

"I'll bring it to her," Alyssa said.

Marta stood in the kitchen, leaning against the counter as Brett and Alyssa used the sliding glass door and stepped onto the porch.

The kids played in the grass, the men sipped on beers as Ian laid out the steak and chicken on the grill.

Nikki lounged on a chair in the sun, Hunter sleeping next to her.

It would have been nice if they'd all stayed in Tower City, but life had a way of moving along, and she didn't mind the direction hers was headed.

She had Ian and her girls.

She had Sadie who pulled into the driveway and bolted inside wanting to hold her baby. She stopped to give Marta a quick kiss on the cheek before joining the others. Ian captured her in a gruff headlock and pressed a kiss to the top of her head before releasing her.

Sadie slapped at him, but she grinned. Like the rest of them, she'd grown up, looked to the future, put in the work to make it happen.

Ian met her eyes through the glass, and he beckoned to her. She joined her friends on the porch and snagged the beer out of Ian's hand.

"Hey," he said, but laughed as she took a swig.

She gave it back, but he set the bottle on the patio table and pulled her close. He nuzzled her mouth with his, and he tasted of beer and sunshine, of love and promises.

The scent of barbecued steak permeated the air on this warm, sunny day.

She leaned against Ian's chest, content.

# NIKKI

Nikki lounged in the shade while Dane sat next to her holding her hand.

Marta and Ian made out near the grill, and Alyssa and Brett played with the kids in the grass.

She turned to Dane. "What did you think when you first saw me?"

He grinned. "You want to know the truth?"

"Yeah."

"I thought you had a great ass."

"Seriously?" She stuck her tongue out at him.

"You asked. And you were carrying all those books. When you looked at me after I took those boxes from you, I lost all thought in my head. A long time ago I told Brett it was love at first sight. I really think it was."

She squeezed his hand. "I feel the same way. I never thought answering your ad would turn into something like this."

"We started something, didn't we?"

"Yeah, we did. I'm sorry about the store. In a way, it brought us together, and it will be sad to say goodbye."

Dane shook his head. "I thought that, but you know what? It wasn't the store, it was running. I would have seen you at an expo, or you would have made your way to race headquarters eventually. We were meant to be together, Nikki."

She met his eyes, the eyes she once described as a gooey Twix bar. They were still the light golden brown with the dark brown edges, and right now they were full of love for her. Sincerity and joy, and maybe not just a little arousal from thinking about her ass.

"You really believe that," she said.

"Damn straight I do. I was looking for something, but I didn't know what it was. I didn't know after I found you either, that what I needed was someone to *do* something. Do something for me, do something about me. Do something to show me how someone can love me. You went into the store that night and that guy knocked you around. You went in because you cared about me, and you wanted to help."

"Yeah, I did. The last thing I expected was Daniel ripping you off."

"The stock didn't matter, but it was a turning point for us, I think. And then we met Liz and you told her off. She said she admired you for that, by the way."

She grimaced. "I'm not looking for her approval."

"No, but you didn't sit there and let her talk shit about me either. And after what I did to you, you still went and talked to my parents, explained what happened. You were in my face from the minute we met—the store's handbook, the social media accounts. You didn't let up, and I didn't know it then, but I needed that."

"You make me sound like a bitch." She laughed. "It wasn't on purpose."

"No, maybe it wasn't, but you made me see I could do better because a woman like you loved me."

"That's sweet."

"Don't ever give up on me, Nik. I'm probably always going to need a good kick in the ass from time to time."

She tilted her head for a kiss, and he pressed his lips gently to hers. "I'll always be here."

"Good, because God, I love you, and I know I wouldn't be able to live without you. You made me try once, and it almost killed me."

"I think you needed that, too."

"Yeah, I did. Probably more than you know." Dane looked over the large back yard. "I'm going to miss these goofballs."

"Me, too. Alyssa and I have been friends forever, but you know, she wasn't moving in a good direction, either. Maybe none of us where. I was chasing men who didn't mean anything to me, Alyssa was hiding. Marta and Brett were trying to run from the way their relationship ended. We've all come such a long way in such a short amount of time. Even Sadie has changed."

Dane looked down at her. "Taking the credit?"

Nikki laughed. "Sure. Why not?"

"Because . . . maybe it's mine. I was the one who needed a store manager."

"I was the smart one who applied."

"But I was the one who hired you."

"Are we going to do this all afternoon?"

"We could, but how about we do this instead?"

Dane slid onto the large lounge chair with her and took her mouth with his.

She wrapped her arms around his neck and let herself sink, Stacy's babies kicking between them.

Maybe they'd both made a few mistakes here and there, but they had the rest of their lives to get it right.

There would always be bumps in the road and hills to climb, but Nikki had good running shoes and a solid partner, and she knew life couldn't get any better than this.

## ACKNOWLEDGMENTS

Thank you to David Willis and Sarah Krewis for giving this novella a quick read for me before publication. It means a lot that I have friends in my corner! I appreciate you!

## ABOUT THE AUTHOR

Vania Rheault has lived in Minnesota all her life. In 2003, she graduated with a BA in English with a concentration in creative writing. When she's not writing, she's reading, playing with her three cats, or going to movie night with her sister.

Find Vania on www.vaniamargene.com and these social media platforms: